Blood Prophecy

Book 2 of the Witch Fairy Series

Bonnie Lamer

ISBN-13: 978-1481953580
ISBN-10: 1481953583

For Xenia, Zuriq, Quinn, Conor and Jadyn.
The loves of my life.

The Prophecy:

A Witch's child of Fae is born
When spirits of the realms are torn.
Into the world, destruction she brings,
While children cry and Angels sing.
None may survive the vengeance of she,
And immortal her soul is to be,
To remedy the world
Of its natural discord.

Chapter 1

"**O**h my God, someone's in my bed!" My brain is screaming red alerts at me as I wake from a deep sleep. It's like a fire alarm going off in my head. Without even thinking about it, I start pulling on the magic from the earth, bringing it inside of me and letting it fill me as if I'm an empty vessel. The feel of it flowing through me, building to a crescendo, is intoxicating. At this moment, as I'm just floating to consciousness, I am one with the earth and ready to safeguard myself with its gift. The magic begins to overflow, wanting to protect me, seeking a target – and then my conscious brain kicks in. Oh crap, it's Kallen I'm trying to maim or kill while I'm half asleep.

"What are you doing?!" he practically yells as he wakes abruptly from a sound sleep. He scrambles off the bed glaring at me. He's wearing gray pajama pants and a black t-shirt that hugs his lean, muscular torso. His black hair is tousled from sleep. He looks really good, even with the death glare.

I mutter a guilty "Oops" as I sit up. "I forgot you were here. I woke up a little nervous because someone else was in bed with me."

"A little nervous? You categorize pulling enough magic from the earth to cause an avalanche – one large enough it could bury this entire house, as being *a little nervous*? Not to mention how heartwarming it is that you completely forgot about my presence."

Okay, this morning isn't off to a great start. "Sorry, I've never had anyone else in my bed before. You shouldn't take it personally."

From the way he's raising his eyebrows and looking at me incredulously, I'm pretty sure he's taking it personally. Kallen is my new Fairy boyfriend. I think. I'm still trying to figure out what our relationship is. He has the black hair and green eyes of the Fae like me, and he's six feet six inches of lean, hard muscle making him absolutely irresistible. But he can also be a condescending jerk sometimes because he's three hundred and fifty human years older than me - though in Fae years, he's not much older than my seventeen. He's working on the jerk thing. I hope he works fast. The one thing I am sure about is he and I won't be having sex any time soon. Apparently, under Fae law, it would mean we're married. I think it's a stupid, outdated tradition, but that's how it is.

Continuing to glower at me, Kallen asks, "Do you think you could let it go now, or do you still intend to use it?"

He means my magic. In all fairness, he does have the right to be worried. My control over my magic is still precarious at best and I could accidently cause a lot of damage. I close my eyes and concentrate on letting the magic flow back down through me to the earth, which it does. Just a couple of days ago, I wouldn't have been able to do this so easily. Kallen would have needed to help me, and that never works out well for him. I open my eyes when I am magic free.

"Thank you." I think he tried to sound like he meant it. He didn't succeed.

Rubbing his hand through his hair, he takes a deep breath to calm himself. "You certainly do keep life interesting. I find I am never at a loss for excitement when I am in your presence." Kallen's speech is always formal, and he never uses contractions. It took me a while to get used to it.

Cocking my head to the side, I ask, "Is that a good thing or a bad thing?"

The corners of his mouth start to curl upwards as he sits back down on the bed. "When I am not in fear for my life, it is a very good thing."

I smile as he leans forward to kiss me. I'm growing really fond of his kisses. Before his lips can touch mine, Mom floats through the door. Mom and Dad are ghosts. Long story short, tragic car accident and they refused to 'go into the light' when they died.

"I thought I heard voices. Your father and I let you sleep in after the week you've had, but now that you're up, we need to discuss what we're going to do about your grandfather." Looking pointedly at Kallen, she adds, "We also need to find appropriate accommodations for your *guest.*"

Mom and Dad didn't hit it off with Kallen when they first met, even though they sent me into the mountains with him to learn how to use my magic. Two other Fairies were trying to kill me at the time, and he was the only one who could protect me, so I guess it made sense. My parents weren't planning on me bringing him back home as my boyfriend, though. They certainly didn't expect me to insist he live with us since he has no place else to go. He gave up his realm to stay in this one with me, so it seems only fair we give him a place to live. At least, it seems that way to me. I suspect Mom and Dad would have said no if they hadn't been in shock last night over how strong my magic has become. I forced my Grandfather, a powerful Witch, from the house when he tried to kill me. They definitely wouldn't have let Kallen sleep in my room if they had not been in shock.

"I do not feel my gratitude for opening your home to me was appropriately expressed last night. I would like to take this opportunity to thank you again," Kallen says. I try really hard to keep my mouth from dropping open. He's not usually so polite. Okay, he's usually haughty and often rude. But he grows on you.

Mom scowls. She doesn't expect Kallen to act like he appreciates anything received from someone who's not a Fairy. He was pretty clear the last time my parents talked to him that he thought Humans and Witches were below him. He was also hung up on the idea he couldn't date anyone who wasn't a full-blooded Fairy. He's undergone a transformation since then, obviously.

"You're welcome," Mom manages, struggling between being polite herself and expressing how she really feels.

Not much has changed with Mom since she became a ghost. Despite being see-through, she's still beautiful with her long blonde hair that I used to love brushing when I was a little girl. Her blue eyes are still bright and get a twinkle in them when she smiles, which she is definitely not doing right now. She's also just as impatient. Turning back to me, she says, "Xandra, are you coming?"

Looking at Mom's insistent, translucent face, I groan. She's not going to leave until I'm out of bed. I'm so not awake enough for this conversation, or for the fact that my mother and my boyfriend look like they're about to have a magical duel. "Mom, I already proved I'm stronger than he is. If he comes back, I'll just do what I did yesterday," I say through a yawn. My confidence in my ability to defend myself with magic has grown considerably in the last few days.

She drags her eyes, which were trying to shoot missiles full of poison at Kallen, back over to me. "Xandra, you have no idea how strong the Witan are. You may be able to take them on one by one, but when they combine their magic, there is no greater force on earth."

My grandfather is the King of the Witches and the Witan is his Witch Council. It's supposedly made up of the strongest and most powerful Witches alive. And they all want me dead. Except for Mom, my biological family sucks. Shrugging, I say, "I guess I'll just have to take them on one by one, then."

"How do you expect that to work out if they all attack at once?" Kallen asks.

Both he and Mom are looking at me with skeptical expressions. Geez, I should at least be able to have breakfast before they gang up on me. I liked it better when they were focusing on each other. Throwing back the covers and swinging my legs over the side of the bed, I grumble, "Fine, I'll get up so we can talk about it."

Relieved, Mom says, "Thank you. Your father and I will be waiting in the kitchen for you." With a last dirty look over her shoulder for Kallen, she floats back out through the door.

Kallen shakes his head as he watches Mom disappear. "I believe it will take some time to become accustomed to living with specters. Providing they allow me to remain here, of course." Turning to me, the smile is back on his face. "Perhaps now I could have that good morning kiss?"

He leans forward and captures my lips with his. When he was going to kiss me a few minutes ago, I thought it would be just a light peck. This isn't one of those types of kisses. This is an open-mouth, dreamy kiss that makes me forget everything else. Moving closer to me, he puts one hand in my long black hair and the other goes around my waist. Snaking my arms up and around his neck, I shift so I'm kneeling and can get even closer to him.

"Ahem." I should have known the moment wouldn't last long. Kallen abruptly pulls away from me and he has the guiltiest expression on his face.

Dragging my attention away from him to my angry dad, I can't help but admire how well Dad has already mastered the 'I'm going to kill you if you touch my daughter again' look. Considering I've never even had a date let alone a boyfriend before, because there are no boys in a fifty-mile radius from our house, he hasn't had any need to use it in the past. This is definitely one of the rare times I'm glad my parents are ghosts. If they weren't, I think Dad's hands would be wrapped around Kallen's neck about now. "I believe your mother told you we're waiting for you in the kitchen?"

I didn't find out until last week that this sandy haired, blue eyed man is actually my stepdad. The fact that he and my mom both have blonde hair and blue eyes should have clued me in, but it didn't. My biological dad is the King of the Fairies and has shiny black hair and bright green eyes like mine—thankfully, the only traits I inherited from him. He is an awful man who seduced Mom to get her pregnant. Then he wanted to kill me as soon as my Witch magic became unbound so he could use my dying blood to open the passage to the Fae realm that was sealed a long time ago. Obviously, my biological dad and I aren't ever going to be close. I consider the angry ghost floating in front of me my real dad.

Ghost or not, I know when he uses that tone of voice, I'd better do what he says. Reluctantly, I stand up. Taking Kallen's hand, I pull him up and we walk towards the door, being careful not to walk through Dad. Not that it would hurt him, it's just too weird. Not to mention cold. Dad follows us as we walk down the hall to the kitchen of our rambling ranch house which sits high in the mountains of Colorado.

My stomach rumbles, reminding me I need food before Mom overloads my brain with new magical knowledge. A week ago, I thought I was just a teenager who lived in the mountains. Now, I know my Mother is a witch, I'm half Witch and half Fairy, and my powers were bound until I turned seventeen. Mom never told me about any of this until my seventeenth birthday last week when my powers became unbound and assassins came for me. I didn't take it well, at first.

I stop just inside the kitchen and open the freezer door, assessing what we have for breakfast. "Kallen, would you like a toaster waffle?" I ask over my shoulder.

His brow furrows. "What is a toaster waffle?"

They don't have processed food in the Fae realm. Or toasters. They can toast things with their magic. I could, too, but since I'm just as likely right now to make the house explode as I am to get my waffle a golden brown, I stick with the toaster. "They're like pancakes but crispier. You cover them in maple syrup before you eat them," I explain as I put four waffles in the toaster slots. "They're delicious."

Kallen looks unconvinced but he says, "I will try one." He takes a seat at the kitchen table and I must give him credit. He's handling the hostility radiating from my parents very well. Last week, he would have made some acerbic comment to make things worse. He was a little bitter then. Forced to come to this realm to assess how big of a threat I was – to this realm and to his. Apparently, his grandmother had a vision that I would intentionally open the gateways between the realms. What she didn't tell Kallen was that I would be able to keep the Fairies in their own realm while sending back the two who were after me. We think she was doing some grandmother matchmaking.

As I wait for the waffles to pop up, I grab some plates and the maple syrup out of the pantry. Mom and Dad are being patient, but I can tell they're itching to get the conversation underway. Using the tips of my fingers, I pull the extremely hot waffles out of the toaster when they pop up and put two on a plate for Kallen and then two on my plate.

I put the syrup under my arm and carry it all to the table. Kallen still looks unsure but he puts syrup on his waffles and takes a bite. They must be to his liking because he keeps eating.

After my first bite of syrupy deliciousness, I look up at Mom. "So, what's the plan?"

Mom and Dad exchange a look and then Dad answers. "We kept you safe from your Grandfather and his minions for seventeen years and we will continue to do so. We need to leave here, find a new place..."

"What?" I interrupt with my fork halfway to my mouth. "You want to run away? You don't want to fight?"

"Xandra, we want you to be safe, and if that means going on the run like your mother did before, then that's what we'll do."

I put my fork down and shake my head. "No. I don't want to run. We don't need to let them chase us out of our home. And besides, if we leave here, we risk people finding out about you." Letting the general public find out that ghosts really do exist just doesn't seem like the smart thing to do. Who knows what chaos would ensue? "I want to stay here."

Mom moves closer and lays her cold hand on my cheek. "Honey, I know you're coming into all this power and you feel like you can take on the world right now, but you have no idea what these Witches are capable of or the magic they can wield. Theirs isn't new magic, Xandra. These are Witches who have dedicated their lives to becoming stronger, more powerful, and they truly are the most powerful creatures in this realm."

I lean back and Mom's ghostly hand drops back to her side. "I don't want to spend my life running because we're afraid to even try to fight! Grandpa's magic was nothing compared to mine. I didn't even feel his magic struggle against me when I was pushing him out of the house last night. I can feel Kallen's magic when he and I practice, so it's not like I don't have anything to compare Grandpa's magic to. I know I'm stronger than he is."

Mom shakes her head sadly. "You caught him off guard, Xandra. That won't happen again. He got a taste of your magic and he knows what he's up against now. He knows how strong you are. He'll be heavily armed with amulets which will protect him from your magic, and I'm sure he'll be working spells well beyond anything I have ever seen before. That's just your Grandfather. There are seven others who will be with him who will be just as prepared."

I glance at Kallen to see what his reaction is. His brows furrow as he watches me and my parents. "Do you think we should run?" I ask him.

"Xandra," Dad says sharply, "this isn't a debate, nor is it a democracy."

Ignoring him, I ask Kallen again, "Do you think we should run?"

His brow becomes smooth and I can't tell what he's thinking. He's doing that thing he does so well where he can keep his face completely free of emotion. I hate it. "I do not know how powerful the Witches your mother speaks of are," he says evenly.

"That's not what I asked you."

Without taking his eyes from mine, he says, "I was not raised to run from a fight."

Dad is in his face in a heartbeat, not caring that his body is deeply embedded in the kitchen table. "I don't care how you were raised or what you think my daughter should do! I have spent the last seventeen years keeping her safe, and no *Fairy* is going to come into her life and take over *my* job and convince her to do something stupid!"

"Jim," Mom says softly as my mouth hangs open, unable to form words. I've never seen Dad do anything like this or seen him this angry. Kallen's face stays blank as he and Dad stare at each other. The tension in the room is combustible and no one seems to know how to end it before it explodes.

Suddenly, Kallen rises to his feet so forcefully his chair falls backwards, shattering the uncomfortable silence. "A powerful being is on its way here."

Dad looks at Mom and all thought of Kallen leaves him as he removes himself from the table and hurries to her side. "So soon?" he asks her.

Mom looks stunned. "No, it can't be. They would need more time to prepare." She looks at Kallen. "Can you tell how many?" The tension of a moment ago now replaced with concern bordering on fear. It's not comforting when my powerful Witch mother is scared.

Kallen nods curtly. "Just one, but this one is very powerful."

"Is it Grandpa?" I ask him. Why can't I feel anyone coming? I'm half Fairy. I should be able to do most of the things Kallen can do. Concentrating, I realize I am feeling something. It's like a tickle at the back of my brain and it's growing stronger. I don't remember feeling anything like this last night when we came home and Grandpa was in the house. Then again, I probably wouldn't have paid attention to the feeling today if Kallen hadn't said something. I would have just put it down to stress. So maybe I did feel Grandpa here and didn't realize it. I really need to start figuring these things out. Apparently, my life may depend on it.

Kallen shakes his head. "No, I do not recognize this magic. I have never been in its presence." Fairies can 'taste' a Witch's particular magic, and once they have the flavor, they begin to acquire immunity to it over time. The process is sped up the more a Witch says the Fairy's name. There are so many stupid magical rules like that; I know I'll never be able to remember them all.

"Would your father send someone ahead to try to take us by surprise?" Dad asks Mom.

Mom looks unsure. "I-I don't know. My father has changed so much since I left." Guilt washes over her face as she thinks about how she had left her home after attacking two guards who were holding her captive for the Witan. I don't think she should feel guilty. If she stayed, they would have forced her to miscarry while she was pregnant with me. According to them, I was never supposed to be born. There's even a prophecy about it with me being responsible for destroying the world. Some people take these things so seriously. Like there haven't been about a zillion other prophecies that the world was supposed to end any number of times in the past. Anyway, I'm happy she escaped from my Grandfather's clutches. I like being alive.

Just thinking about it causes magic to flow back inside of me. How dare they come and attack us in our own home after all they've already put my mother through. The magic feels good as it fills me, and I don't have any problem containing it, keeping it from overflowing. Rising to my feet, I walk out of the kitchen with my parents and Kallen following in my wake.

"Xandra?" Mom says nervously. "What are you doing?"

I turn around to look at both of my parents. "I'm facing whatever they're throwing at us. Dad, I know you want to run, but I can't. I won't live in fear. If this past week taught me anything, it's that I need to be strong enough to protect myself and the people I love. If I am going to survive in this world, I have to start by standing up against those who want to kill me simply for what I am." Through Dad I see Kallen standing with his feet apart and his arms crossed over his chest. I still have a tough time guessing what he's thinking, but I think he's supportive of my decision.

Turning my back on all of them again, I walk to the front door. Kallen has pulled his own magic and I feel it just barely touching mine. Not in a challenge, but as if he's adding his strength to mine. A smile touches my lips, but I don't turn around. Throwing the front door open, I thrust my magic forward in search of the Witch who dares to attack us.

I don't know who I expected, but it definitely wasn't the person at the end of the
driveway. As my magic surges forward, a slightly plump, very pretty woman who looks to be in her early sixties, which I wouldn't have guessed except for her long graying hair, falls to her knees. She raises her arms above her head and then brings them back down to her sides. As she does this, a visible shimmering shield falls into place just as my magic hits her. Witch magic isn't usually this visible, so I can't help but be impressed, but I don't falter in my attack. If my magic gets to her, it will cause pain that burns from the inside out. With her head bowed, she puts her hands out in front of her as if trying to hold the shield in place against the onslaught of power I've flung at her. I feel the shield buckling. It's strong, but not strong enough to keep me out for long.

"Quillian!" the woman shouts. "I mean you and your daughter no harm! I've come to help you."

"Xandra, please stop," Mom whispers quietly next to me.

I glance over at her to see if she's serious. "Do you know her?" I ask, but I haven't lessened my attack yet.

Mom nods once. "She's my mother."

Chapter 2

O h, great. Another blood relative. I'm sure this is going to go well. Have I mentioned how they all seem to want to kill me? With a sigh, I stand down. I don't let my magic go back to the earth. I pull it back inside of me so I'm ready to defend myself if necessary. If I wasn't so on edge, I would spend a moment marveling over how much control I have when threatened. Why don't I have this much control when I'm trying to do everyday things?

Kallen comes to my side and he takes my hand in his. "Are you sure this is wise?" he asks Mom.

"No."

Again, comforting. But I guess I would give Mom the benefit of the doubt, too, if I were in her shoes. Then again, she hasn't held me prisoner and threatened to kill my child. Before last week, I never would have used the term dysfunctional to describe my family, despite the fact that my parents are ghosts. This week, it seems the only way *to* describe it.

"Why are you here?" Mom asks the woman who is still kneeling in the driveway. That must be really cold on her knees since she's only wearing a pale pink suit with a blazer and a skirt. It looks like it's made from wool, but still, not appropriate mountain wear. Or fending off magic wear.

Looking uncertainly at me, Grandma slowly rises to her feet as the shield which kept my magic from burning through her slips away. Her resemblance to Mom is obvious now that I'm paying attention. Her hair may be graying, but you can still tell it's the same rich, silky blonde as Mom's was. But the real giveaway the two are related is the vibrant, ocean blue of their eyes. I always wanted beautiful blue eyes like that, but I got the black hair and green eyes of my father. I'm not complaining, I just wanted to look more like Mom growing up.

I also wanted grandparents growing up. Dad's parents died when he and my Aunt Barb were in college and obviously, I never knew Mom's parents. I thought they were dead. I dreamed of baking cookies with Grandma and going fishing with Grandpa, typical Grandparent stuff. I never imagined they would be powerful Witches who want to kill me. I guess you really do have to be careful what you wish for.

"As I said, I'm here to help you," Grandma says as she brushes the snow from her reddened knees. "I tried to talk your father out of coming back here, but I was not successful. He's back home, preparing with the Witan. I'm here to stop him from doing something he would regret for the rest of his days, provided he survives at all." She looks sideways at me as she says the last part. Hey, it wasn't me who started this whole mess.

"Why now?" I ask because Mom is looking a little shell shocked. "Way back when, you were pretty eager to kill me just like him."

Several emotions wash over Grandma's face. I don't know her, but they kind of look like a combination of guilt, shame, and remorse. I'm not ready to rely on her body language or facial expressions just yet, though. She may be a really good actor.

Looking sadly at Mom, she says, "I have always regretted my part in forcing you to flee. When I told your father you were pregnant and the details about the night with the Fairy, I thought he and I would help keep your secret. Perhaps hide you ourselves if anyone ever guessed what had happened. Most of all, I thought we'd protect you from the ignorant fools he surrounds himself with. I had no idea he would react the way he did."

Mom snaps out of her stupor and she looks mad. The kind of mad that makes you really glad it's directed at someone other than you. To Grandma, she says accusingly, "But you didn't do those things. You were going to let them kill my child."

Grandma shakes her head. "No, Quillian. I pled your case to the Witan and to your father. I begged them to spare your child. But they wouldn't hear me. They were fools who could not see past their own fear." She pauses, trying to swallow back her emotions. "My faith in your father was shattered that day." She looks pretty angry herself now as she continues. "I was formulating a plan to flee with you when news came that you had already left on your own. I have never forgiven myself for not telling you of the preparations I had made for our escape. I was horrified that you were out in the world with no place to go, no money, and unable to use your magic for fear we'd find you. Every day since the day you left, I feared I would never lay eyes on you again. I have missed you so much, Quillian." Tears are streaming down Grandma's face now.

"My name is Julienne, not Quillian. I left that name behind when I stripped away any ties to you and Father." Grandma winces but doesn't say anything. She looks too choked up to say anything. Oh, please. I'm still not buying it.

My brows furrow now as I think about what Grandma said. Okay, maybe I'm missing something here. "You stayed with Grandpa all these years even after supposedly losing all faith in him? Who would stay with someone who did something so awful to his daughter? But you did. That makes it kind of suspicious you'd show up here offering to help us fight him, don't you think?"

Grandma's face hardens as she looks at me. "I stayed because I held out hope your mother would come home. I stayed for her."

Yeah, right. I must have mumbled that out loud because Kallen gives my hand a gentle squeeze and his mouth has curved into a smirk. Guess he thinks it sounds fishy, too. I turn to Mom and she looks like she doesn't know what to believe. Dad looks like he wants to punch Grandma in the face. When did he become so violent? I'll add that to the list of crimes my biological family has committed. They're quickly turning my Dad into a sociopath.

As things have calmed down some, I feel my hold on my magic start to slip. Magic doesn't like to be stagnant. Very soon, I need to either use it or let it go. If I don't, it may try to seek its own target. Apparently, that last part's not normal for anyone except me. Kallen's theory is that I pull more magic than anyone else due to my dual heritage, and that much magic in one place becomes combustible. I'm a time bomb right now, and my ticker is rapidly counting down to zero.

Kallen feels me losing control. "I believe it wise to decide to either hear her out or fend her off." He gives Mom a pointed look and then looks at me. Mom catches on pretty quickly. Last night while we had a quick bite to eat before going to bed, I only mentioned briefly that I have trouble controlling my magic, but I stressed it with a couple of examples.

Looking back at Grandma, Mom says, "We'll give you the benefit of the doubt. For now." She turns her back and floats through the front door. Apparently, Grandma's supposed to follow her into the house. I like this less and less as each minute goes by.

Grandma's eyes follow Mom and a single tear slides down her

cheek. I wonder what caused it. The fact that the daughter she helped chase from her life is now a ghost, or that Mom doesn't trust her? Either way, I guess it sucks to be Grandma right now.

Kallen, Dad and I hang back for a minute. I need to take a breather and make sure I have control over my magic. I need to let it all go because I haven't quite mastered the ability to keep a small amount of magic inside of me for extended periods of time like Kallen can. It's kind of all or nothing for me right now. Closing my eyes, I begin to push the magic back down towards the earth.

Kallen interrupts my concentration by saying, "I believe your mother is being foolish."

Great, that's a fabulous way to help me calm down. I glower at him as I say, "I thought you were going to stop insulting my mother."

"He's right." I know shock is written all over my face as I turn to look at Dad. His arms are crossed over his translucent chest and a deep scowl is lining his brow. "We gave your grandfather the benefit of the doubt and he tried to kill you in our kitchen. If that woman has been so eager to find your mother, why didn't she come with her husband when we called for help?"

I hadn't thought about that, but Dad has a good point. Why is Grandma just now showing up?

"Do you believe her to be a Trojan horse?" Kallen asks Dad.

I need to lessen the tension of the situation somehow and humor seems the way to go. "Wait, you were born around that time, weren't you? So, you probably got to see the Trojan horse close up, right?" I tease. Kallen seems to disagree with my humor idea.

He narrows his eyes at me. "I am not quite that old in Cowan years. That was a couple of thousand years before my time." Cowan is the term the Fairies and Witches use for humans.

I shrug and smile. "Too bad. It would have been pretty cool if you had."

Kallen rolls his eyes but I can see him trying to suppress his own smile now. "Perhaps we should concentrate on this moment in time instead of when I was born?"

"Fine." I sigh dramatically because I really don't want to deal with Grandma. But we shouldn't be leaving Mom alone with her, either. "Okay, let's go talk to Grandma." If there was any less enthusiasm in my voice, I could pass for a mortician. I turn towards the door and since I'm still holding his hand, I pull Kallen along with me.

In the living room, Grandma is sitting on the red, overstuffed couch with her hands primly in her lap, and Mom looks grim as she appears to be sitting in the recliner. Neither of them is speaking and the air is so thick with tension, I expect it to start dripping down the walls. Figuring I can't make it any worse, I decide to ask Grandma Dad's question. "Where were you when Grandpa came here? If you were so eager to see Mom, it seems like you would have come with him."

A dark shadow passes over Grandma's face. "Your Grandfather neglected to tell me your parents had contacted him. I heard nothing about it until my assistant overheard a conversation between two members of the Witan. When I called your Grandfather to demand he tell me where to find you, he was already on his way home. He told me what happened. He thought it would make me believe he had been right all these years, but I told him he was still being a fool. I hung up, packed, and caught the first flight here."

"How could he keep it from you if you live in the same house?

Wouldn't you have known Mom called? Or that he was leaving?" I push. Even in the mountains, we have caller ID, and I would notice if someone in the house left for a few days. She's telling a good story, but nobody in the room is ready to believe her yet. Especially me.

Grandma looks down at her hands still folded in her lap. "The property is very large, and Sveargith and I have had a marriage in name only these last eighteen years. I live in the guest house now and our paths rarely cross anymore. We used to be so in love, your Grandfather and me, but he threw that away when his heart hardened against his daughter." Looking up at Mom, she says, "He didn't just break your heart, Quillian. I'm sorry, I mean Julienne. He broke mine as well, and I will never forgive him for either sin."

I catch Dad rolling his eyes and shaking his head as he watches the emotions pass between the two women who haven't seen each other for a lifetime, my lifetime to be exact. Mom's starting to look like she's caving. Dad thinks so, too. He sighs in disgust. "Julienne, don't be taken in by these lies. Your father apologized, claimed it was all a big mistake, that he wished he could take it back, and then he tried to kill your daughter."

"I know." Mom whispers. She still looks like she's caving.

Grandma wrenches her eyes from Mom to look at Dad. "What can I do to convince you I am telling the truth?"

Kallen answers before Dad has a chance. "There is a simple way." All eyes are on him, now. We're all eager to have this settled once and for all, and for me, that means Grandma gets the boot sooner as opposed to later. Looking at Mom, he says, "You insisted I take a blood oath before you entrusted Xandra to my care. You can do the same with your mother."

Hey, that is a good idea. I forgot about the whole blood oath thing. Another thought hits me. Kallen is still bound by the blood oath he made with me. He must protect my life as he would his own. If I die, so will he. Is that the real reason he stayed? Because he's still bound by the oath to keep me safe? Oh, we're definitely talking about this after we get Grandma squared away.

Grandma inclines her head towards Kallen, and a small, tight smile touches her lips. "An excellent idea." Her expression doesn't quite match her words, though. Is she nervous about doing this? Good, then she's probably one step closer to being out the door.

Mom ignores Grandma's reaction and turns to Kallen. "In the closet of my and Jim's bedroom, on the top shelf, is the ceramic bowl and a knife. You should be able to reach them easily. Xandra, please show him the way."

I'm torn. I don't want to leave my parents alone in a room with someone we don't know if we can trust yet. Mom has her magic to defend herself, but Dad doesn't have a drop of magical blood in him. Who knows what Grandma could do to him, even if he is a ghost.

The outline of a grim smile touches Mom's lips as she senses my hesitation. "It's fine, honey. I have taken the same precautions inside the house as I have outside."

Mom has the outside of the house booby trapped, much to my surprise last week. She was able to fend off the first attack of the Fairies with an invisible Fairy trap and exploding Witch's bottles, which are totally gross. She put iron nails in a bottle with her urine and buried them in the ground around the house. Now, all she must do is say an incantation and they explode out of wherever she has them hidden. And they must be hidden well since neither me nor my little brother Zac have ever found them.

Thinking of Zac causes a little ping in my heart. Before I left for the mountains, he and my Aunt Barb left for Denver to wait out this whole mess. They'll come back home when it's safe, and I want that to be soon. Thinking about it gets me all riled up again and I shoot Grandma a dirty look because she's the only one I can vent on right now.

Reluctantly, I show Kallen where my parents' room is. I open the closet door and another ping hits my heart. Mom and Dad's clothes are still in the closet. No one has ever brought up the idea of getting rid of them since they don't really need them anymore. I guess it would be an acknowledgement of the fact that they don't belong to this plane of existence anymore and they never will again. We've tried not to focus too much on that over the last three years. We've all pretended it's perfectly normal to have your parents be ghosts. It's amazing what we can teach our brains.

Kallen pushes a few boxes aside on the top shelf and finds the ceramic bowl we used when he took his blood oath. Aunt Barb must have tried to hide it when she put it away. Maybe she thought the Fairies would be able to do something with it, I don't know. Kallen hands the bowl to me as he reaches up for the athame. It's a double-edged knife with a sharp point and it looks old. It's made of silver and the handle has intricate designs that I'm sure mean something, but I haven't had the chance to ask Mom about it. It's a pretty cool looking knife, though.

Kallen puts the knife in the bowl and then puts his hands on my cheeks. "This will all work out. You are strong enough to take on a hundred Witches, if necessary."

I don't think he means that literally, but it is nice of him to say it. He ducks his head to give me a kiss and without thinking I take a step back. Words jump out of my mouth as if they had been waiting on the tip of my tongue for my lips to open so they could make their escape. "Did you stay because of the blood oath?"

He's definitely not keeping his face blank now. Torrents of emotions are washing over it as quickly as a blink of an eye. First, I see confusion, then understanding, then incredulity, and finally, anger. A lot of anger.

Crossing his arms over his chest, he looks down his nose at me from his immense height. I hate it when he does that. It makes me feel really small. "You still do not trust me," he huffs. "After coming here to save you, after giving up the chance to return to my home and my family, you still do not trust me. And, just to make you aware, blood oaths do not travel from realm to realm. If I had returned to my own realm, I would have been free of any responsibility for keeping you alive. I could have left and never looked back or troubled about you ever again. It is only within this realm my life is at risk if I do not do everything in my power to save yours."

Oh, I didn't know about the crossing realms thing. Now I feel terrible. But instead of saying I'm sorry, my mouth says, "Why didn't you tell me that before?" I think I may have more trouble controlling my mouth than I do my magic.

His eyes narrow and his face is granite. "I did not think it necessary. I thought the reason I stayed was quite clear, but apparently this time I was the naïve one. What an unusual twist for us." He takes the bowl and athame from me and starts walking towards the door.

"You didn't have to be such a jerk about it. I was just asking." See, no control whatsoever.

Kallen turns back towards me, and he still looks really mad. He opens his mouth to make what would probably be a cutting remark, when Dad comes in. Taking in our faces and the emotions filling the room, his eyebrows rise. "Trouble in paradise?"

"No," I lie. "Dad, are you going to follow us around the house whenever we leave a room?"

With a chuckle, Dad says, "Possibly, but I actually wanted to ask Kallen a couple of questions this time." It's good to see a smile on his face, but I'm getting really tired of the guys in my life laughing at me, which I hope I'm conveying with the dirty look on my face. Kallen is still glowering at me as well.

Ignoring what's going on with us, Dad asks Kallen, "Is there a way to, I don't know a better way to say this, cheat when taking a blood oath?"

Kallen nods. "In a way, yes. The wording is very important. For instance, the blood oath I took," he pauses here to narrow his eyes accusingly at me again," I swore to protect Xandra's life as I would protect my own. If I had decided that the only way to keep her from opening the gateway between realms was to sacrifice my own life, I would not have had to protect her life." Now that he's said the words out loud, he actually has the decency to look a little sheepish as he admits that to my dad. He came to this realm believing he may need to do just that, but he eventually figured out I'm on his side.

Dad crosses his arms over his chest as he looks evenly at Kallen. I think he's going to pounce on what he just said as a reason to tell Kallen he can't stay, but he doesn't. Apparently, he's too preoccupied with the current dilemma to think about it. "Are there any spells or amulets or anything magical which could be used to negate a blood oath?"

Kallen thinks for a moment then shakes his head. "I have never been told of one, but Fairies have not been in this realm for several hundred Cowan years. It is possible I am ignorant of some magical charms or spells that may have been discovered to prevent the binding of the oath. I doubt it, though. The magic is incredibly old and strong."

I'm still feeling snippy, so I'm tempted to make a comment about him admitting he's ignorant about something; it so rarely happens. But I don't because that would be mean. This whole argument was my fault in the first place for thinking he had ulterior motives for staying here. "Do you think Grandma is going to try to weasel out of the blood oath?" I ask Dad. I hadn't even thought of that. Dad is thinking about all this way harder than I am apparently. Then again, he's had eighteen years to think about what ifs. I've had a week.

Dad shrugs. "Let's just say I believe anyone capable of allowing their daughter to be held captive while others determined the fate of her child may not be the most trustworthy person. From what I know of your grandparents, I believe caution is wise."

Great, now we can't even be sure a blood oath will really tell us if Grandma's telling the truth or not. Pulling my bottom lip between my teeth, I rack my brain for a better plan. Turning to Kallen, I ask, "What happens if a Witch and a Fairy make a blood oath? Could the Fairy magic involved in the oath prevent a Witch from using a spell or anything to make it not real?"

Kallen's brows draw together. "It is likely, but as you are only half Fairy, there is no guarantee your Fairy magic would work that way."

I roll my eyes. "I figured that out myself, thanks." Okay, I'm still a bit snippier than I should be. "I meant, what if Grandma made a blood oath with you?"

Dad and Kallen are both looking at me like I'm either crazy or stupid. It better not be the latter. Kallen speaks first. "How would a blood oath with *me* force your Grandmother to protect *you*? I realize you have not had much magical training, so I will explain. A blood oath is supposed to be between the two people who are directly affected by the oath." There's that lovely condescension of his again. Yup, he still has a lot to work on if we're going to date. At least I don't feel badly about being snippy now.

"I'm not a moron, thanks. I figured that out all by myself as well. But, if you are already sworn to protect me as you would your own life, couldn't the blood oath be worded so that Grandma would agree to help you protect me? Sort of like a backup plan? Protect you as you're protecting me or something? Then it would be your Fairy magic against her Witch magic."

Dad looks impressed and Kallen almost looks shocked. "That is actually a very good idea."

"I do have them from time to time," I say dryly.

Looking hopeful, Dad turns to Kallen. "Do you think it would work?"

"If worded correctly, yes, I believe it would."

Dad looks relieved now. "Do you think you can do it?"

Kallen looks confident now that the idea has sunk into his brain. "Yes."

"Great, let's get this going then. The sooner we decide what we're doing about that woman, the better."

I suspect Dad would be happier if it turned out Grandma does have something up her sleeve. He's definitely not going to be as forgiving towards her as Mom seems to be, even if this turns out in her favor. He has a determined look as he floats out the door and back towards the living room.

I begin to follow him, but Kallen puts his hand out to stop me.

He still looks upset with me, but he leans down like he's going to kiss me. He doesn't kiss me, though. Instead, he pushes my hair away from my ear and whispers, "I stayed because I wanted my body to be in the same place as my heart, *despite* the oath." With that, he turns and strides out of the bedroom with the bowl and the athame.

Okay, did he just tell me he loves me, or am I reading too much into his comment? If that is what he meant, this was a heck of a time to tell me. Not only were we arguing, but we're right in the middle of dealing with this whole grandma mess. And am I in love with him? I've never been in love, so I really don't know what it's supposed to feel like. I know I like him. A lot. But love? With a heavy sigh for all the confusion and emotions piling up in my life, I follow Kallen back to the living room.

Dad must have already announced what we talked about because Mom is looking unsure and Grandma looks furious. She practically shouts, "You expect me to make a blood oath with a Fairy?! That's outrageous! Fairies can't be trusted! That's why they were banished from this realm!"

I give Grandma a hard look. I definitely don't have any warm and fuzzy feelings for her and insulting my boyfriend certainly isn't going to create any. I reply to her, trying extremely hard to keep my anger in check. "I don't know about all the rest, but Kallen is trustworthy. And I know *he* wants me to stay alive." Implying I'm not sure she does. I really hope she caught that.

The right corner of Kallen's mouth hikes up slightly in a half smile. I think I may have just made up for my blood oath question earlier. I slide my hand in his in a show of solidarity and he wraps his fingers around mine. I try to give Grandma a withering look, but I'm not sure I'm successful. She doesn't look intimidated at all. She still looks livid.

"Xandra, dear, I'm sure you believe that, but isn't your mother's experience with Fairies enough to show you their true nature?"

Okay, maybe holding Kallen's hand may not have been such a good idea, because now, he's squeezing mine like he's trying to pop a water balloon. Owwwww. I think he's trying to hold back from starting a magical confrontation with Grandma, so I try not to complain. "Do not presume to know my nature. I am a Sheehogue Fairy and we have never had a quarrel with Cowans nor Witches. It was my grandmother who worked the magic to close the realms, protecting Cowans and Witches alike from the Pooka Fae. It was also my grandmother who sent me here to help protect Xandra and keep the realms closed to each other. So you see, there is no doubt in anyone's mind what *my* or *my grandmother's* intentions are. Xandra is unable to say the same about her grandmother."

There are two types of Fairies in the Fae realm – the Sheehogue and the Pooka. The Sheehogue are 'live peacefully with every-one' kind of Fairies, and the Pookas are 'who can I bully today' kind of Fairies. My biological dad is a Pooka and he was willing to kill me to open the realms. They really aren't very nice.

I'm pretty sure that Dad's chuckling only adds to the sting of Kallen's words because Grandma's face is bright red. But who cares about Grandma, maybe there's hope for my parents liking Kallen after all. At least Dad, anyway.

After taking a deep breath, which I doubt helped, Grandma says between tight lips, "I apologize if I offended you and your kind." Your kind? That's just a tad bit insulting, and I don't think it's going to win her any points with Kallen. "I have been told tales of Sheehogue intervention between the Pooka and the humans on occasion. But I also understood from these tales that the Sheehogue prefer to remain neutral and are not prone to intervention unless the situation becomes dire. So, you can understand my assumption that you are of the Pooka Fae. I did not realize the situation had reached the point where the Shee-hogue would intervene." Wow, that was not the world's greatest apology. I wonder if Kallen is aware that I like to have the use of all my fingers, not just the ones that aren't being crushed in his grip right now.

"I have heard tales of Mrs. Smith's treatment at the hands of you and your husband. I personally witnessed your husband try to kill Xandra. Therefore, you can understand my hesitation to believe you to be anything more than a distraction while your husband gathers *seven* other Witches to take on *one* Witch Fairy."

Grandma's eyes flash. If it turns out she is on our side, I don't think she and Kallen will ever bond after this exchange of words. "Yes, I can understand why you are hesitant to trust me. It simply took me by surprise that I would be making a blood oath with a Fa...with you." Oh, good catch on her part.

Dad crosses his arms over his translucent chest, and he has a 'don't mess with me' expression on his face. "That's the deal, At-hear. Take it or leave it." I didn't know Dad even knew her name, as he's been calling her 'that woman' for the last half hour.

Glancing over at Mom, I wonder why she's been so quiet. That's not normal for her. She always has something to add to a heated conversation. I've also never seen her bite her nails before like she is right now. I wonder if she can change the length of her fingernails by biting them. Do they feel solid to her? Does anything feel solid to her? I'll have to ask her later. We haven't talked a whole lot about what Mom and Dad can feel. Again, part of that trying to seem normal thing we've had going on. We just pretend everything's the same for them as it is for the rest of the family.

Straightening her shoulders, Grandma says, "I will make a blood oath with whomever you would like. I am here to help."

"Are you sure, Mother?" Mom asks quietly. There's the implication in her question that she believes her mother may not be telling the truth and will suffer the consequences of the blood oath. Which is always death. I wonder how a person dies from a blood oath gone wrong. Do they just drop dead from a heart attack or stroke or something wherever they're standing? Or is it some kind of slow painful death? I'll add that to my list of questions to ask later. It kind of ruins the effect if I seem ignorant about what is going on.

"Yes, Quillian, I am."

"Her name is Juilienne," Dad practically growls.

Grandma inclines her head towards him. "Of course. You will have to excuse me. It will take some getting used to on my part, but I will adjust." Turning to Mom, she says, "Are we ready to begin?"

Before Mom has a chance to respond, Kallen says to her, "If you do not object, I would like to set the terms of the blood oath."

Mom's brow furrows. I don't think she's a hundred percent on board with this plan, but she knows she's outnumbered if she disagrees with it. She nods at Kallen and says, "Okay." She turns towards Grandma. "Mother, please take the knife and add your blood to the bowl."

Grandma looks down at the bowl and knife for the first time and her breath catches. She looks back up at Mom. "You are using your athame for a blood ritual?" Apparently, athames are never supposed to draw blood.

"It's a little late to be concerned about that." Mom says pointedly. She had to stab two guards instead of using her magic to escape my grandparent's house. "It has already shed blood, a little more will not taint it any more than it has been already."

Grandma looks down at the athame once more. Is that a tear in her eye again? Over a knife? Or is she feeling guilty about what Mom had to do to escape. I hope it's the latter. I would hate to have my opinion of her drop even lower.

Picking up the knife, she holds the index finger of her left hand over the bowl and uses the tip to cut her skin. Several drops of her blood fall into the ceramic bowl without making a sound. She turns and hands the knife to Kallen. He has no hesitation about using the athame to draw blood. It doesn't seem to be a thing for Fairies. He repeats the process and his blood joins Grandma's in the bowl.

"Speak the words of the oath," Mom directs him.

"By this blood, let Queen Athear Levex join me in my oath to protect Xandra Illuminata Smith from harm or death, whether by magical, natural, spiritual, Cowan, blood relative or any otherworldly means. This binding will forsake previous loyalties forged by blood, marriage, debt or friendship." Looking over at Dad and me briefly, he continues. "If we choose to sacrifice our own lives for our cause, our dying breath will be spent in an effort to fulfill the promises set forth with this binding." Turning back to Grandma, he adds, "Let the laws of the Sheehogue take precedence over Witch law in concerns to this binding, and let the Witch and Fairy magic come together as a force to hold this oath true and unable to be unbound by either." Grandma's eyes spark when he finishes, but she doesn't say anything.

Mom hesitates for a moment but then with her mouth in a grim line, she closes her eyes. When she reopens them, she speaks the words that joined Kallen and me in our blood oath. "Bound by blood, moon and tide, by this oath you must abide. If by traitorous heart you deceive, or by lack of courage you mislead, count that breath to be your last, as the earth will claim its next repast."

I'm just about to think how much I like Fairy magic better because it's more visible, when I hear a sizzling sound and a puff of smoke rises from the bowl. "What was that?" I ask as I peer around Kallen to see what happened. The mixed blood has turned a strange shade of amber. And are those sparkles? What the heck? That's not supposed to happen. Nothing visible is supposed to happen.

It's Mom's turn to give Grandma an accusing look. "Did you attempt to nullify the oath?"

Grandma closes her eyes and sighs. "No, I did not." Opening her eyes, she says firmly, "That is what happens when a Witch and a Fairy form a blood oath."

That didn't happen when Kallen and I did ours, but then again, I'm only half Witch. Still, I turn to Kallen whose face has become blank as he and Grandma link eyes. "Is that true?"

Kallen takes a moment to answer me, his eyes never leaving Grandma. "It can," he says vaguely. More firmly, he adds, "The oath is complete."

Dad doesn't look like he believes him. Yeah, me neither. Something's fishy here. With doubt in his eyes and a frown on his brow, Dad asks, "Are you sure?"

Kallen finally tears his eyes from Grandma to answer Dad. "I am positive." His face is still a blank page. Grandma has tiny worry lines around her eyes, and it's obvious she's trying to school them. Something is going on between her and Kallen, but I have no idea what. I give Kallen a puzzled look, but he ignores me. Oh, I really don't like that.

Dad still doesn't look convinced, either. He turns to Mom. "So, what, now we're supposed to just welcome her into our home? I don't like this, Julienne. There is something going on with *that woman*," he flings his arm towards Grandma, "that I don't trust."

Kallen is standing stiff as a board, not reacting to Dad. His eyes have moved back to Grandma's. "What's going on?" I hiss quietly, trying not to clue Dad in on whatever is happening between Kallen and Grandma.

He finally tears his eyes away from her again and deigns to look at me. It's about time. "All is well."

On the list of all the crap answers he's given me over the last week, this is the biggest. This is my life we're playing with! But there's something about the set of his jaw that tells me I'm not going to get a better answer than that right this minute.

I huff and turn towards Mom. "What now?"

"I would like you and Kallen to get your Grandmother's bags from the driveway. Your father and I need to talk to her."

I expect Dad to object since he has that murderous sociopath look on his face again, but he doesn't say anything. I guess Grandma's staying then. Great, I'm so excited. Maybe we can get to the cookie making part of our relationship sometime. If she doesn't decide to kill me first, that is.

Without a backward glance at Kallen, I walk to the front door and go outside to get the suitcases sitting in the snow at the end of the driveway. Grandma had apparently taken a cab up the mountain. That must have cost her a fortune. Good, I hope it did.

Kallen catches up with me and puts his hand on my arm so I'll stop. "She is telling the truth. She is here to help."

I pull my arm out of his grasp and whirl around. All the frustration from the last hour comes pouring out at him. "Really? Just how do you know that? Because some blood smoked and sizzled and you and Grandma made eye contact? Forgive me if that isn't enough to make me want a group hug with the two of you. I'm a little too selfishly concerned right now with keeping myself alive. I figure one of us should be."

The hurt on his face quickly turns to anger as he lets his arm fall back to his side. "I thought I heard you say that you trust me. I must have been mistaken."

"So, what, I'm supposed to have blind faith in you? Even I'm not that naïve."

He has shuttered his face now so I can't tell what he's thinking or feeling anymore. "Is blind faith such a terrible thing when you claim to care about someone?"

Ignoring his attempt to guilt me into compliance, I ask, "Are you going to tell me why you suddenly think Grandma is one of the good guys?"

His mouth sets in a thin line and it takes several heartbeats for him to answer. "There are some things that should be explained by the person who holds all the answers."

"Enough of the stupid cryptic speak. Between you and Mom, I've had enough of it to last me a lifetime! Are you going to tell me or not?"

"I can tell you she took a significant risk making that blood oath with me."

"Oh, well, that clears everything up. Thank you." Where's my sarcasm napkin? I seem to have some dripping down my chin.

Kallen runs a frustrated hand through his hair. "Xandra, I am sorry. I cannot tell you."

"Cannot or will not?"

"Cannot."

"Why not?"

"Because I'm bound by Sheehogue law."

"Are you trying to make me hate you? Because you're on the right path if you are."

His frustration is almost palpable now. "Xandra, I am not deliberately keeping anything from you."

I snort. "Funny, it feels like you are."

Kallen hangs his head. Something I haven't seen him do before. He's always been too proud to do something like this, so it can't be a good thing that he's doing it now. "I made a mistake when I set the guidelines of the oath."

Uh oh. That sounds ominous. I almost expect to hear the duh duh duhn music start playing. Maybe I really don't want to know what he's keeping from me. "You made a mistake?"

"Yes."

I wait a minute expecting him to continue, but he doesn't. "What kind of mistake?" I prompt.

"I weaved Sheehogue law and magic into the oath because I was certain your grandmother was not the Witch she claimed to be. That would have exposed her lies. Instead, I stumbled into an ancient law by mistake. I am now bound by it."

"Kallen, that doesn't make any sense at all. What ancient law?"

He closes his eyes as he runs his hand through his black hair, leaving it deliciously messy. Though, it's not delicious enough for me to lose track of the conversation. "Well?" My arms crossed over my chest now, I'm tapping my foot impatiently. Wow, I think I just moved one step closer to turning into my mother.

Opening up his pleading eyes, he says, "Xandra, I need you to trust me. Please. Your grandmother is not going to hurt you. She cannot."

I growl in frustration. "So now we're back to the blind faith thing."

He crosses his own arms across his chest now. "Have I given you reason not to trust me?"

Hmm, that's a trick question. He didn't exactly tell me his true purpose for coming to this realm when we first met, but he didn't really lie to me either. But it was an awfully thin line between the two. Technically, no, he didn't lie to me and he did have my best interest at heart, as well as his own. I look up at his bright green eyes that are so vibrant and beautiful – I don't think there's a color in nature that could compete. Right or wrong, I'm going to put my faith in him. I've trusted him with my life before, I guess I'm going to have to do it again. "Is she really bound by the blood oath?"

Relief washes over Kallen's face as he realizes I'm acquiescing. "Yes, she is. Her intentions can only be pure. She would suffer greatly if not."

What is that supposed to mean? I doubt I'm going to get an answer, so I don't even bother to ask. "Fine, but you're carrying her suitcases."

His lips curl up into a sexy smile. "As always, I am a slave to your desires." I roll my eyes, but I can't help smiling. That's just not playing fair. He's hard to stay mad at when he decides to be charming.

Sobering again, I ask, "You're absolutely sure Grandma's on our side?"

"I am."

I look at him for a long moment until he raises his eyebrows in question. In my heart, I know Kallen wouldn't say it if he didn't believe it. If Grandma's not on our side, then she has Kallen fooled. But he's pretty sharp when it comes to anything magical, so he'd be awfully hard to fool. Sighing, I say, "Then I believe it, too."

He puts his hands on my waist and pulls me to him. "Thank you for trusting me." As I snake my arms up and around his neck, he lowers his lips to mine in a mind-blowing kiss that tells me just how glad he is I decided to put my faith in him. But in the back of my mind, the thought that Grandma's still hiding something takes root, and I intend to find out what it is.

Chapter 3

"**A**nd you wonder why I follow you two around."

I groan as Kallen quickly ends the kiss and takes a step back, dropping his hands from my waist. I turn around to look at Dad, expecting the same reaction from this morning; but to my surprise, he looks more amused than mad. Maybe he really has decided he likes Kallen. That doesn't change the fact that he's made a habit of interrupting our kisses, though.

"We were just coming back in," I grumble.

"It might be difficult to carry the bags and walk to the door with your lips locked like that."

"Dad, really?" My face turns what I am sure is magenta or maybe even maroon. This is not my life. It's not bad enough I have people trying to kill me, now I need to add dealing with my dad making bad jokes about me kissing my boyfriend as well? I've only been up for an hour, but I'm ready to go back to bed already. Maybe it's not too late to wake up from this nightmare. "Aren't you supposed to be talking to Mom and Grandma?"

The smile washes off his face and the grim set of his jaw tells me he didn't like how the conversation went. "I don't believe this is a good idea. I'm worried about letting that woman into your life."

I nod glumly. "Yeah, me too. But it doesn't seem like we have much of a choice." I glance at Kallen out of the corner of my eye to see if he takes that comment as lack of trust in him. I think right now he's focusing more on his own embarrassment about Dad catching us kissing again. His cheeks seem a little redder than normal, too. Awww-he's so cute like this.

"That may be true, but I still think it's wise to take precautions." Dad has always been a pragmatist. "If trusting Athear turns out to be a mistake, I don't know if your mom has it in her to stand against her own mother. Over the years, she has always clung to the belief that her mother had not agreed with your grandfather and his minions, and Athear has played right into that. Even if she could stand against your Grandmother, I'm afraid she won't have enough power to hold both of us in this plane and still wield enough magic to fend off an attack by a Witch who, according to her, is much more powerful than she ever was."

Well, at least my parents are telling me the truth now, whether I want to hear it or not. They kept a lot of secrets from me over the years. Maybe that wasn't such a terrible thing after all. "That's not very comforting, Dad."

He shrugs in a helpless gesture. "I know." Then his eyes move to Kallen. "That's where you come in."

Kallen raises his brows in question but doesn't say anything. Dad clears his throat before speaking again. He's a ghost; I'm assuming he doesn't have phlegm, so it must be a stalling thing. Finally, he says, "If someone had told me an hour ago that I was going to say this, I would have pronounced them insane right on the spot." Dad was a doctor before he was a ghost. He could have done that. "I want you to be glued to Xandra's side–every minute of the day." He stresses the last words.

It takes a moment for his meaning to sink in. "Every minute?"

Dad's expression hardens and it seems to take some effort for him to smooth it back out. "Yes, every minute."

"Okay." Is he serious?

"I heard what you said this morning. You said your grandfather's magic didn't even show up as a blip on your radar when you forced him to leave the house. But you said Kallen's magic is strong enough to at least give you a challenge. If he's truly that powerful, then he just became your own personal bodyguard."

My brows come together. As much as I like the part about Kallen sticking to my side, I don't like the part where Dad thinks I need a bodyguard.

Dad must see that on my face. "Humor me, kiddo. I'm worried about you and it would make me feel better knowing someone powerful is watching your back."

Guess I can't really argue with that. It makes me feel better that Kallen is watching my back, too. "Okay, I get it."

Kallen has been remarkably quiet while Dad and I have gone back and forth. I'm surprised; he usually has an opinion about everything. Dad turns back to him and he has an amused smile on his face now. "I'm assuming this is okay with you?"

Kallen inclines his head in agreement, and there's a smile trying really hard to form on his lips, but he won't let it. He's trying to look solemn. At least, his is until Dad says, "I expect you to be a gentleman."

Okay, now I'm quite sure Kallen's biting his tongue. Literally. Really hard. To say he's offended is an understatement. Obviously, Dad doesn't know how seriously the Fae take sex. I wonder if that's a Fairy thing or just a Sheehogue Fairy thing. I haven't asked. But it doesn't seem like the Pooka have morals about anything, so I'm guessing it's a Sheehogue thing. My list of questions just keeps getting bigger and bigger. I think I'm going to need to carry a notebook and pen around and start writing them all down because I'll never remember them all.

"Do I have your word?" Dad pushes.

I don't know how Kallen says it through a jaw clenched as tightly as his is, but he manages to say, "Yes."

Dad nods once and chooses to ignore the fact that he obviously insulted Kallen. "Alright then, I'll see the two of you inside." He turns and starts floating towards the house. When he's about fifteen feet away, he says over his shoulder, "Kissing is fine, just not when I'm around, please." I'm pretty sure he's chuckling when he floats through the front door because his shoulders are moving up and down.

I refuse to acknowledge the flush of red surging into my face because of Dad's parting words. Instead, I turn back to Kallen. "I'm impressed you were so quiet after he said that. I expected to feel you pulling magic any second."

Visibly trying to relax his facial muscles, he says, "Even though I have never been accused of being anything other than gentlemanly, I thought it best to let your father have his say. I am a guest in his house."

"Are you really the same guy who showed up naked in the woods last week? Cause you're certainly not acting like him. I think I liked that surly, sarcastic, not afraid to say what's on his mind guy better. This guy," I move my hands up and down to indicate all of him, "is kind of a pansy."

He gives me a sharp look until he sees the twinkle of teasing in my eyes. "Is that so?"

I sigh and nod my head wearily. "I'm afraid so."

In a blink of the eye, he growls as he puts his arms around my waist, and I squeal a little as he picks me up off the ground with my arms pressed against his chest. He plants his delicious lips on mine, proving he is far from boring. As our tongues dance in perfectly choreographed movement, the rest of the world falls away. For a few glorious moments, my mind is free of everything except this kiss.

He ends the kiss slowly and then slides me down his body until my feet can touch the ground again. "Still prefer the surly, sarcastic guy? Because I can bring him back."

I smile and shake my head slowly. "He had his moments, but I guess I don't miss him as much as I thought I did. Actually, now that I think about it, I definitely like this Kallen better."

Kallen grins as he picks up Grandma's bags – a large suitcase, a vanity case, and a garment bag. She sure packed a lot for a spur of the moment trip. "I am not the biggest catch for hand-fasting in the Fae realm for nothing. No one can resist my charm." Then he strides towards the front door on his long legs, leaving me marveling at his self-assurance. The worst part? He actually has reason to be that cocky. He is powerful and gorgeous and is a full-blooded fairy. I can only imagine how many other Fairy women were throwing themselves at him. I really don't want to know. Yes, I do. No, I don't. Wow, I'm so jealous. Why I'm jealous of Fairy girls he may have dated before and forgot all about when he chose to stay here with me, I don't know. I just am.

Pulling my attention away from watching Kallen's lean muscular body move gracefully like a large cat as he walks back to the house, my eyes are drawn to the large picture window in the living room. Grandma is standing there staring at me and looking worried. I assume she's wondering if Kallen told me her secret. I'm sure she'll be happy to find out he didn't.

Chapter 4

When I follow Kallen into the house, Grandma is already unzipping her suitcase. Geez, you'd think she'd at least wait until she was in the guest room. It starts to make more sense when I see what she's pulling out. Apparently, it wasn't just clothes that she packed.

"What is all this?" I ask, looking over the things she has set on the coffee table.

Grandma looks up from what she's doing. "I'm sure you are familiar with some of these items, and I'll explain the others..."

I hold up my hand to cut her off. "Before you start making assumptions about what I know and what I don't, you should just assume that I don't know it. I didn't even know magic existed until last week, and the only magic I've used since then has been my Fairy magic."

Grandma's eyes are as big as platters. "You didn't know that magic exists?" She turns her dumbfounded expression towards Mom, and if ghosts could blush from embarrassment, Mom would be.

"I thought I was keeping her safe from the magical world. I had no idea that as soon as she turned seventeen, the Fairies would come looking for her." Grudgingly, she adds, "If Kallen hadn't taught her to use her Fairy magic, she may not have survived."

Whoa, Mom used Kallen's name. She must be ready to trust him if she's not worrying about saying his name anymore. If we survive the next few days, maybe everything will work out between him and my parents. That's a big IF on the surviving part.

Grandma moves her eyes to Kallen. "You must have taken quite a risk coming here to fight against your own kind."

"It was the Pooka who came to this realm to do harm. They are neither my kin nor my *kind*," Kallen replies evenly.

Grandma has the decency to look at least a little embarrassed by her insult. Inclining her head, she says, "Of course. I apologize for not distinguishing between you being a Sheehogue Fairy rather than a Pooka."

Returning to the conversation about my magical ignorance, she asks me, "You have not used any type of spell?"

I shake my head. "No." Then I remember the healing spell Mom and I did for Kallen. "Unless you count the time Kallen was hit with a nail from Mom's gross pee bottles. Mom worked the actual spell and Aunt Barb mixed the plants for the salve. I really didn't do much. The only thing I did was combine my saka with Mom to make a mana." I stumble over the unfamiliar words.

Grandma smiles. "I believe you mean using your mana to create a saka."

Okay, so I'm not going to pass the pop quiz on magical terms. "Can we just call it magic like the Fairies do? It's a lot less confusing that way."

Grandma nods and says kindly, "That is an excellent suggestion."

"When we combined our mana...I mean magic," Mom corrects

herself, "to heal Kallen from a wound created by iron, I was not a strong enough vessel to channel her magic. Once it was focused on his wound, I had to let go."

Grandma looks confused. "What do you mean you were not a strong enough vessel?"

"Xandra's magic burns hot and fast," Kallen explains. "She draws more magic than any other magical being I have ever encountered. It cannot be channeled by another without causing physical harm; it feels like being burned from the inside out. It is also impossible to contain it if she loses control." He glances sideways at me. I'm certain he's remembering vividly all the times he tried to contain my magic. I give him my best 'I'm sorry' look.

Mom nods in agreement. "She healed his wound almost instantly."

Grandma looks stunned as her eyes float back to me. "Healed? Completely? I've never heard of such a thing; iron does massive internal damage to a Fairy. How is that possible?"

I shrug. "I just did what Mom told me to do. I visualized his wound healing. Then it healed."

Grandma shakes her head. "Unbelievable. You are certainly a remarkable young woman." She pats the spot next to her on the couch. "Please, join me and I will explain what I've brought with me."

I hesitate. I'm still not feeling warm and fuzzy about her and the idea of sitting next to her on the couch is not thrilling. What if one of those things is a Witch Bottle like Mom has planted all over? Who knows what god-awful things this stuff could do to me? I glance at Kallen who is now leaning one shoulder against the far wall with his arms crossed over his chest and his feet crossed at the ankles. He looks so good I almost lose my train of thought.

As if reading my mind, he says, "It is all defensive magic."

"Xandra, give your grandmother a chance, please," Mom rebukes gently.

"Fine, it's just my life we're playing with," I grumble under my breath as I walk to the couch.

"And I have every intention of keeping you alive," Grandma says with what I would probably think was a nice smile if I wasn't so on edge. Right now, she's not going to win me over with a smile. She doesn't seem to realize that because she's still smiling even though I'm sure it's written all over my face that I don't trust her. I sit down next to her anyway. Well, not next to her, I sit at the other end of the couch so there's at least two feet between us, but we're on the same piece of furniture.

"Why don't we start with something simple," Grandma says, picking up a small leather pouch. "We'll make a mojo bag for you to wear. It will help protect you from magic that could do physical harm, deflecting the attack back towards the Witch responsible."

My brow scrunches. "You mean like Witches' bottles?"

Grandma nods. "Yes, if a Witch bottle explodes around you while you are wearing the mojo bag, it will flare to life and put in place, for lack of a better word, a force field around you. It then sends the spell back to the one who used it. However, mojo bags may only be used once, so it will be necessary for us to create several of them."

"Okay," I say taking the leather pouch she's holding out to me. "I'm supposed to put stuff in it?" Kallen smirks and I shoot him a dirty look. He takes great amusement in my magical ignorance.

Grandma doesn't make fun of me, though. Okay, that's one brownie point for her. "Yes, you will put an assortment of items in it that are known for their protective properties. Then you will say a spell which binds their collective power and holds it until needed. This is considered low magic – magic that invokes an item's natural power. It's also called Earth magic."

Hmm, and I thought Kallen was a walking encyclopedia of Witch magic. She's explaining things nicer than he usually does, but Grandma is making me feel like I'm in school. I hope the entire day doesn't go like this. I'm better at learning by trial and error rather than by boring lecture. Though, my trial and error with magic has led to some disastrous consequences. Maybe I should just shut up and pay attention.

Looking at the assortment of herbs, stones, jewelry, and other things I can't name, I attempt to speed this along. "What first?"

"You will need to use several herbs and stones. The first will be yarrow. It'll provide protection as well as boost your self-confidence."

"She is definitely not lacking self-confidence. You may want to start with something that will lessen her self-confidence," Kallen teases from his position against the wall.

Other than me throwing him a quick dirty look, Grandma and I both choose to ignore him. "The yarrow is the feathery looking leaves right there." I pick up the leaf she's pointing at and put it in the bag. She then has me put in nettle and vervain leaves, whatever those are, and a small onyx stone. The last item is a pinch of salt. I hope that doesn't mean I'm going to have to eat this stuff.

"Now, cinch the bag closed and you will recite the protection spell." Turning to Mom, she asks, "Where might I find your grimoire?"

My face turns bright red when Mom says, "I no longer have it."

Grandma is shocked, to say the least. Apparently, a Witch is naked without her grimoire. "Did you lose it in your travels?"

"No, I did." I confess. "I caused an avalanche and it got buried in the cave Kallen and I were staying in at the time.

Now Grandma looks really confused. "Avalanche? Cave?"

"The details aren't really important, are they?" Dad asks impatiently. "Can't you just write the spell down for her?"

"Of course." Trying to recover her composure, Grandma searches her purse for a pen and a small pad of paper. Once she finds them, she begins to write. When she's done, she hands it to me. "Now, just hold the bag close to you and while saying the spell imagine a defensive wall coming up around you."

"Okay." I take the paper and look it over skeptically. It's not like I'd know whether it's the real deal, though.

I open my mouth to begin but Kallen interrupts me. "You may want to move away from her," he says to Grandma. His mouth turns up in an amused smirk again. I really want to stick my tongue out at him, but I refrain. I don't even comment back like I normally would. I let my eyes do the talking.

Grandma looks at him impatiently. "I'm sure I'll be fine." Turning back to me, she says, "Go ahead, dear."

It seems appropriate for me to stand up because I feel like I'm giving a formal presentation, or an audition, since all eyes are riveted on me. Taking a deep breath, I imagine a cinderblock wall all around me and begin to read, "*Herb and stone, heart and mind, with my will may all combine. Protect my body, my life, my soul, from forces dark who strike first blow. Evil magic based in sin, sent back before it can begin. Those in my heart will be unharmed, by this Witch's protective charm.*" And then there's a loud explosion.

Grandma is suddenly across the room in a heap, right under where there used to be a picture window and next to where there used to be a door. Now, a couch is embedded in the wall. The coffee table must have gone out the window because it just isn't around anymore. The recliner is sticking out of the fireplace.

I'm taking all this in through the haze of a transparent, cinderblock wall that forms a six-foot perimeter around me and goes up to the ten-foot ceiling. My eyes search for Kallen, hoping I haven't hurt him, but he's standing in the same spot with a smug smile on his face.

"Guess that answers that question," he says triumphantly.

It takes my befuddled brain a minute for that to make sense. I look at the paper that is still in my hand and see it- *those in my heart will be unharmed.* Ooooohh. Blood rushes to my face as I realize my subconscious just told us both how I feel about him. Instead of acknowledging it, I ask, "What happened? It wasn't supposed to do this, right?" Okay, I know that's a really stupid question, but my mind is a little fuzzy right now.

Kallen chuckles as he pushes himself off the wall. "No, it was not."

I turn to Mom to ask her what I did wrong and her mouth is in a perfect o. I don't think she knows what happened either. Dad looks really freaked out. Kallen seems to be the only one who isn't in shock, or unconscious. "What went wrong?" I ask.

He walks to me, still laughing and shaking his head, and puts his hands on my shoulders. "Nothing went wrong, my little Witch

Fairy. You did everything correctly."

I look around at the destruction that used to be our living room. "Then why does the house look like a tornado stormed through it?" I should probably go and check on Grandma, but I'm a little scared to go near her after tossing her across the room. So, I'm going to assume from afar that she's fine. She seems to be breathing okay.

Kallen chuckles again. "How aptly put. You are a tornado personified."

The shock is wearing off and now I'm getting annoyed. "Will you please just answer my question?"

"This," he sweeps his hand out to encompass the room, "is what happens when what should have been a gentle summer breeze is replaced by a tornado."

I still don't get it. I'm probably being obtuse, but good lord, I just blew up the living room! I'm a little bit overwhelmed right now. Narrowing my green eyes, I look into his. "If you don't stop laughing at me and answer my question, I'm going to blow you up next."

Of course, he doesn't take me seriously, but he does answer my question. "The average Witch would be the gentle summer breeze. The spell would be cast, maybe a few sparks would be evident and then the mojo bag would be properly stored for future use and the Witch goes on her merry way. But if you replace the gentle summer breeze with a tornado, YOU, instead of simply a small spark occurring, what is created is a spell so large it cannot be contained by a tiny little leather pouch. Therefore, instead of being stored, the spell is cast out. And where a normal Witch would have created a thin wall around herself, your wall is a hundred times thicker and needs more space. To make room, it removed all obstacles except for those you specifically told it not to harm."

"Oh." What else is there to say?

"Are you saying she can't perform spells? She is half Witch," Mom says. There's some defensiveness in her voice.

Kallen turns his eyes to her and Dad, who have not moved from where they were floating before I worked the spell. He shakes his head. "No, I am saying that the outcome of a spell Xandra casts will be a hundred times greater than it was intended to be."

"And you couldn't have said something before she worked the spell and destroyed the living room?" Mom's voice isn't defensive anymore, it's angry.

Kallen inclines his head. "Would you have believed me if you had not seen it with your own eyes?"

Mom's lips move as if she's about to say something, but apparently, she thinks better of it. After a moment, she finally admits, "No."

Across the room, Grandma begins to stir. Her eyes open and she takes in the room, and then her eyes turn to me. Is that concern in them – or fear? She tries to stand up, but it seems her ankle must have gotten twisted and she sits back down. "So much power in one so young is dangerous," she says to the room.

"I did warn you," Kallen points out.

Grandma gives him a tired look. "Yes, you did, but my pride wouldn't listen." She smiles weakly. "I'm lucky it didn't get me more than a twisted ankle and a headache."

"If it had been a truly dangerous spell, I would not have let you teach it to her."

Placing my hands on my hips, I look up at him. "What do you mean, you wouldn't *let* her? Just because you were the first one to teach me things doesn't mean you have full rein over my magical education."

Both of his eyebrows rise, and I know he's going to say something condescending that's going to make me even madder. "What basis from your vast magical experience will you use to determine if a spell is safe or not?" Okay, he has me there, even if he is being a jerk again. Before I can say anything, he continues, "It makes more sense for someone who is versed in Witch magic, and has experienced your magic firsthand, to determine the ramifications of a spell spoken by you."

I scrunch my face up in what I hope looks like disgust. "You know, my father is right over there." I nod my head in Dad's direction. "I don't need another one."

"Believe me, I have absolutely no desire to be your father." The curve of his lips and the fire in his eyes tells me he really doesn't want to be my dad. Again, a blush crawls up my neck to my face. Now I'm flustered and tongue tied, which I'm sure is what he intended.

Dad clears his throat in the awkward silence. "Yes, well, now that you've established you only have one father, I'll give my opinion. I believe Kallen is right. He has the best idea out of all of us what you are capable of, so he should have final say in what spells you do." Great, the father/boyfriend bonding has continued and created a brain trust that will decide what I can and cannot do. They can go back to hating each other any time now.

I glare at them both, but Kallen looks amused and Dad pretends not to notice. Continuing, he says, "But, before any of that is decided, we need to figure out what we're going to do about the door and the window. It gets awfully cold in these mountains at night." Of course, he and Mom don't have to worry about it, but the rest of us do.

Turning to Dad, Kallen is a little less cocky, but still self-possessed. "If Xandra will let down her wall, I can reverse the damage she has done," he says, making me sound like a five-year-old who broke a lamp and now he has to clean it up. He and I are going to have a long talk about his attitude when we have some time alone. Or maybe I'm just being too whiny and defensive because of my magic going all wonky again. Yeah, probably that.

Grandma looks at him doubtfully. "You are able to perform reversal magic?"

"Yes, I am."

Grandma actually looks impressed now, though she's trying hard not to. I look away from her and turn to Kallen. "Can all Fairies do that?" If so, maybe I can do it, too. It would be nice to be able to clean up my own messes.

He shakes his head of silky black hair mussed by the explosion, its only effect on him. His hair looks even better than before. I'd love to run my fingers through it. But I'm going to ignore that desire right now. I need to focus on the situation at hand. Besides, it would be more than a little awkward with my parents and grandmother right here.

"No, it is quite difficult to perform reversal magic. It requires a lot of power and refined skill," he says. "The only other Fairy I know who can do this is my Grandmother."

My lips purse together as a thought hits me. "So, you could have reversed the avalanche and the rockslide I caused?"

He shakes his head, looking amused at my expense again. "You created natural disasters on a grand scale. There is no magic strong enough to reverse that. Now, as impressive as it is you have held this wall in place for so long without another magical mishap, I cannot reverse the damage until you let it go." Again, I'm five and he's scolding. Yeah, we may still need to have that talk even if I am being whiny.

Letting that idea go for the time being, I take a minute to marvel over my accomplishment here. Honestly, I hadn't even realized I'm still holding enough magic to keep this wall in place. Kallen told me I would learn to do this, but I didn't think it would happen any time soon. I smile proudly, which causes some eyebrows to rise in my direction. I don't care. I may have destroyed the house, but I learned something about myself in the process. I am capable of control.

Kallen cocks his head to the side. "Care to share with the rest of us what is making you smile so?"

"No," I say sweetly. He narrows his eyes at me, but I ignore him as I concentrate on letting my magic go.

That turns out to be easier said than done. I haven't really had to pull back magic that is creating a solid object, transparent as it may be, back through me before. And trust me, this wall is solid. The problem is it wants to stay put. I know that sounds strange, but my magic seems to have a mind of its own sometimes. Kallen once told me the only other person he ever heard talk about magic as if it is sentient is his grandmother. I wish I could meet her someday because she sounds interesting. That probably isn't going to happen since I'm never, ever going to the Fae realm. I'd be a walking target there.

Okay, Kallen's impatient look reminds me of what I'm supposed to be thinking about. I try doing what I normally do and imagine my magic sliding back to the earth. But it won't go. Maybe if I take a deep breath, close my eyes, and clear my mind of everything else. I focus only on my magic. I love how it feels flowing through me, so warm and calm. I let it wash over me as I reconnect my conscious mind to my subconscious that has been holding the wall in place. That quiet hum in the back of my mind. Not an annoying hum, but a pleasant, calm hum, like a monk meditating. It becomes louder. As I delve deeper into the magic within me, it feels as if it's singing to me now. Like the sound of my mother's voice singing a lullaby. My magic will take care of me. It'll soothe my soul from the stress it has felt. It'll wrap me tightly in a cocoon of love, keeping me safe, guarding my body and mind. All I need to do is hold onto it, burrow into its arms, my haven from the woes of the world. My sanctuary. Just hold it close, don't let it go. It'll teach me of its power, its wild abandon that will bring me happiness as I surrender myself to it.

Ow. Ow! What is that? This isn't peaceful. This hurts. My magic isn't comforting now – there's too much power. It's overwhelming. It's giving me a headache. And what was that? Oh, that's just annoying. Not only is my magic causing too much pressure inside of me as it tries to ooze out my pores, but now there's something on the outside pushing against me. Like I don't have enough to deal with right now. Oh, wait. I recognize that magic. I've tasted it before. Kallen. If he's using his magic against me, that can't be good. Something about this cocoon I've wrapped myself up with must be wonky for him to do that. It never works out well for him and I promised I wouldn't hurt him like that anymore.

I must take control back. I control the magic. It doesn't control me. This is not how I save my family and Kallen from becoming targets in my fight. If I don't have control, I'm as dangerous to them as my enemies are. I pull the magic back, like I'm playing tug of war and I have the strongest people on my side. I feel it diminishing, struggling, but losing. I'm pulling it back through me and shoving it back into the earth. As the wall falls, Kallen's magic comes rushing towards me. I must stop it. If I don't, it'll burn through me like I'm being scorched from the inside out. It may not burn as hot as mine, but it still burns. So, I'm going to gently push back, keeping our magic a line of molten lava where they interact, but not burning through either of us. After a moment, I feel his magic pulling back. He senses that I'm in control again.

When I feel the last drop of magic leave me, I open my eyes. Wow, I thought the living room looked bad before. Now it looks as though it has been set on fire and then extinguished. Several times. Oops.

Chapter 5

I search for Kallen, hoping I didn't hurt him again. He's kneeling on the floor about ten feet away from me, panting. His skin has an ashen pallor and it takes him several minutes to catch his breath.

"You did it," Grandma breathes from where she is standing next to the window with what looks like a bucket of water. She must have been trying to put the curtains out, because a small flame starts up again, startling her. She uses the last bit of her water to put it out.

I drop to my knees in front of Kallen. I expect him to be angry, to back away from me. Instead, the corners of his mouth start to move up, but they only make it to a half smile. He manages to say, "Always...interesting...around...you."

A small laugh escapes me as I recall our conversation from earlier. I put my hand on his cheek. "Did I hurt you?"

He turns his head slightly so he can kiss my hand. "Not this time. But you have tired me a great deal. I have endless pity for whomever you release that magic of yours upon."

"Xandra, are you alright?" Mom asks with a tremor in her voice.

I turn to look at her and am about to ensure her that I am, when I realize Dad isn't next to her. Oh god, where is he? "I'm fine,

Mom. Dad…?" I leave the question hanging because I'm not sure I want to finish it.

"He's fine," Mom assures me. "I sent him outside when it all began."

"When what began?" I ask Mom but I'm looking at Kallen.

He lifts his arms and puts his hands on my shoulders. "When you began to set the air on fire."

"What?!" That's not possible. "I did not."

It takes him moment to take in enough oxygen to explain. I half expect Mom or Grandma to jump in, but they wait for Kallen to do it. "You did. You pulled so much magic around you that it was competing for space with the very molecules of the air. You created an imbalance."

I remember him explaining imbalances to me. Suddenly, I feel ill. "You said only black magic practitioners create imbalances."

Kallen shakes his head. His breathing is slowly returning to normal. "No, I said practitioners of black magic create imbalances on purpose to draw as much power as they can. You created an imbalance because you temporarily lost control of your magic. It is not the same."

"Why did Dad have to go outside?"

Hesitation washes over his face. After several heartbeats, he finally says, "Because the imbalance you created did not affect only our plane of existence."

I don't understand. "How could I affect another plane of existence while in this one? They should have been safe, shouldn't they?"

Finding her voice again, Mom answers this time. "No, honey. We do exist in another plane, an in-between place, not here and not where we'll eventually go. This plane is only separated from yours by a hair's breadth, which put your father in danger as he can't protect himself as the rest of us can. Though, I was starting to believe we wouldn't be able to protect ourselves, either," she says, and I can't tell if it's despair in her voice or fear. Probably both. Great, my mom's scared of me. "If Kallen wasn't here..." She shakes her head. "This is all my fault for keeping so much from you. We would have been safer if I had taught you the ways of magic as you grew up."

My mouth is still open from the first part of what she said. It's insane. They're ghosts, how could I hurt them? I turn back to Kallen. "Am I that dangerous?" Please say no.

"Yes."

My face falls and I stare at a singed spot on the floor. Kallen places a hand under my chin and lifts my face until our eyes meet. "But you are learning control. It was not me who brought you back from wherever your magic had taken you. You did that. I only lessened the damage while you took control back. Now, I can reverse the damage."

"Okay," I say quietly. I felt so powerful a few minutes ago and now I feel defeated. How can I fight off my enemies if I will end up hurting my family and Kallen in the process?

Kallen pushes himself to his feet. He's a little wobbly, but other than that he seems okay. He holds his hand out to me and I let him pull me up, though I'm not the least bit tired from having that much magic flow through me. "Perhaps you could make your grandmother a cup of tea while I clean up." He kisses me on the cheek and lets my hand go.

I nod and give Grandma a half-hearted smile. "Would you like tea?"

"That would be lovely." Her smile is about a hundred watts brighter than mine. "I'm afraid using magic tires me out quicker these days than it used to." She starts walking toward me with a slight limp, making me remember that she injured her ankle when I threw her across the room, knocked her out and almost set her on fire. I bet she's really happy she came to help, now.

I walk over to her and put her arm around my shoulders and my arm around her waist. "Let me help you," I murmur. It's the least I can do since I'm the one who caused all of this. We walk slowly to the kitchen.

"I'll let your father know it's safe for him to come back in," Mom says, and she floats towards the place where the door was. If she wasn't a ghost, the couch I flung at the door would keep her from going outside. Since she is a ghost, she floats through it with her blond hair gently flowing behind her. Are those singed marks on the ends of her hair? I don't think ghosts get split ends, so they must be.

I help Grandma into one of the chairs at the kitchen table and then I fill the tea kettle with water. After lighting the burner underneath it, I get a mug out of the cupboard. From the pantry, I get a couple of different boxes of tea to give Grandma a choice. "We used to have better tea when Mom still drank it," I explain, "but Aunt Barb and I aren't as picky as Mom was. I'm afraid we only have Earl Grey and Orange Ginger Mint."

Grandma smiles again. "I would love a cup of Earl Grey." As I get her tea ready, she says, "Your friend is quite extraordinary. I've never met someone who could wield such magic - except you, of course. He's quite handsome, as well. I can see why you're drawn to him."

Drawn to him? What am I, a moth? "But you hate the fact he's a Fairy, right?" I ask and I'll admit there's some accusation in my voice.

Grandma shakes her head. "No, but I am worried about his influence over you."

I whirl around to face her. "What's that supposed to mean?"

Grandma falters a bit, trying to find the right words. Finally, she says, "I'm afraid I've never met a Fairy who wasn't looking to gain from helping another. It's not their way to be altruistic."

I'm about to tell her what she can do with her opinion of Kallen when a lightning bolt hits me. "What do you mean you've never *met* a Fairy who wasn't out for their own gain? Fairies have been locked out of this realm for over three hundred years. Are you saying there are other Fairies here besides Kallen?"

Grandma's face turns pink and I can tell she's about to do some backpedalling. "I misspoke, I have never *heard* of a Fairy who was not out for his or her own gain."

The kettle starts to whistle, and I turn to make her tea, giving myself a moment to resist the temptation of drawing magic and kicking her out of the house like I did Grandpa. She definitely has secrets. Big ones. And I want to know what they are. I suspect my life may depend on it. I take a deep breath before I turn around and ask, "What ancient Sheehogue law was woven into the blood oath that Kallen can't tell me about?"

When I peer at her over my shoulder, Grandma suddenly becomes busy straightening her pink wool skirt that now has little scorch marks on it. "I'm sorry, dear. I have no idea what you're talking about."

Uh huh. Sure she doesn't. I bring her tea to her and put it down so hard that some sloshes over onto the table. "You know, keeping secrets from me isn't the way to make me trust you."

"Again, I don't know…"

I shake my head. "Don't even bother denying it. You aren't telling us the whole story, and until you do, I don't care what Mom thinks. I'm going to consider you a temporary ally at best."

Grandma looks at me for a long time before she speaks. "I know life has not treated you well as of late, so I understand your suspicion, but not all secrets kept regard your safety. Some secrets are too big to tell."

I roll my eyes. "In other words, you don't care what I think; you're not going to tell me. Gee, glad you came to visit. How soon did you say you'd be leaving?"

"Xandra!" Mom exclaims from behind me. "You should be more respectful to your grandmother."

I turn to give Mom an incredulous 'Really?' look. "Sorry Mom, but I'm not buying her innocent act. I don't consider anyone keeping secrets from me right now as being on my side."

Mom looks like she's about to scold me again, but Dad cuts her off. "Julienne, you can't let your feelings take precedence over your daughter's safety. Xandra has every right to be leery, or have you forgotten it was just yesterday her grandfather tried to kill her?" I like how Dad keeps throwing that out there so no one gets too caught up in this whole family reunion thing.

Mom's pale lips press together in a thin line. She's spared having to reply by Kallen coming into the kitchen. "It is done," he says to no one in particular.

Wow, he looks terrible! There are dark circles under his eyes, and he looks like he's about to fall down. Between trying to keep my magic in check and reversing the damage I did to the house, he must have exerted a tremendous amount of energy. My face scrunches up into a frown as I watch him lean his back against the wall. "Oh my god, Kallen. You look like you should be lying down."

"Are you alright?" Dad asks with true concern in his voice.

Kallen nods weakly. "I will be fine if I rest for a short while."

Dad turns to me. "Why don't you take him to your room so he can lie down?" With a guarded look at Grandma, he adds, "I think you could use a little time away from our guest, as well."

He certainly doesn't have to tell me twice. I can barely suppress the relief I feel at the idea of getting even a few minutes away from my grandmother. I nod and take Kallen by the hand to lead him to my room. I bite my tongue so I don't say anything that will get someone talking and we won't be able to make our escape, however brief it may be.

Kallen practically flops onto my full-size bed, which does not accommodate his length well, and closes his eyes. Pulling my bottom lip between my teeth, I ask, "Are you alright?"

He opens one eye. "I would be much better if you were lying here next to me."

I smile and climb onto the bed so I'm lying on my side facing him and prop my head on my hand. "I guess that means you're not *too* tired," I tease.

I let out a small yelp and laugh when he rolls me onto my back with him on top of me. He holds himself up with his elbows to keep most of his weight off me. "Perhaps I am faking fatigue to have a few stolen moments with you." Mmm, I like the sound of that. But I don't believe him. "It is amazing how you can make flannel sleepwear look good."

Oh god, I forgot we're still in our pajamas! With everything that's happened since we got up, fashion has been the least of my worries. I have on loose fitting baby blue flannel pajama pants and a matching form fitted long sleeve tee. Nothing revealing, but still, they're my pajamas. "I guess we should get dressed."

"Soon," he says and then his lips are on mine. I wrap my arms around his back, and I revel in his touch. One of his hands buries itself in my hair, and the other starts to explore. I can't help a soft moan as his lips kiss a trail along my jaw to just the right spot on my neck. I don't even care if Dad comes in. This feels way too good to make Kallen stop.

"You are so beautiful," he murmurs just before his lips find mine again. I pull him down so his body is flush with mine, supporting his weight so I can deepen the kiss and let my hands roam just a little bit. Now, it's his turn to moan.

All too soon, his lips leave mine and he leans his forehead against mine. He's breathing heavily again, and it has nothing to do with being tired from using so much magic. "You are going to drive me to distraction. Perhaps your father was not wrong in insisting I act like a gentleman, for I find when I am this close to you, I want to be anything but gentlemanly."

I smile – hopefully, a sexy smile. "I don't want you to act gentlemanly."

With a loud groan, he rolls away from me to the other side of the bed and closes his eyes. "You are not helping," he complains. "My restraint is precarious at best right this moment. I prefer not to have your father find us in a compromising position."

"Fine." I roll onto my side and prop myself up on my elbow again. With my other hand, I trace soft circles on his chest. "And you thought you were the only one who's irresistible," I tease.

He opens one eye and raises his eyebrow. "No, I did not. I am fully aware of how irresistible you are. Otherwise, I would be back in my realm being adored instead of here where you do not do nearly enough of that."

I pinch him hard on his chest and he opens both eyes now and flattens my hand against his chest so I can't do it again. "Ouch, why would you do something so mean?" he asks in mock outrage as if he didn't just try to make me jealous.

"I've heard enough about your Fairy groupies for the day."

He chuckles. "You are even more beautiful when you are jealous."

A simpering smile plasters itself on my face. "You know, I haven't given the whole groupie thing a try. Maybe after we take care of Grandpa, I should explore that option and get some of my own. You do make it sound appealing."

With a feral growl, he's back on top of me in a flash. "I prefer your adoring crowd to be limited to one."

I laugh. "Oh, so it's okay for you to make me jealous, but you can't take it?"

"I am not jealous," he says haughtily. "I simply believe you have too much on your plate right now to think about locating and keeping the interest of a male harem."

I raise my eyebrows. "Harem? I like the sound of that."

With a low growl, he kisses me again, deep and thorough. Apparently, all thought of Dad floating in is lost from his mind. When he finally lets me come up for air, I grin against his lips and say, "Okay, maybe I don't need a harem after all."

Rolling back to the other side of the bed with his eyes closed and a satisfied smile on his face, he says, "I thought you would see it my way."

I take one of the pillows and hit him in the face with it. "You're still a pompous jerk."

He takes the pillow and places it under his head. "Yet you still hold me in your heart."

Okay, I'm really tempted to pinch him again. "You were awfully sure of that when I performed the spell earlier, weren't you?"

He opens his eyes again and turns his head towards me. "I hoped that was the case. I was pleased to have it confirmed."

Lying on my back again, I take his hand in mine. "What am I going to do if I can't control my magic when Grandpa comes?"

"You gained control of it this afternoon."

I snort. "Barely."

Kallen gives my hand a squeeze. "Neither barely nor heartily changes the fact that you did gain control."

I shrug. "I guess not."

We're silent for a few minutes and then I hear his soft even breathing. He has fallen asleep.

Chapter 6

Kallen only sleeps for about twenty minutes. I take the opportunity to take a quick shower and then pull on some jeans and a red turtleneck sweater. I might as well be clean if this ends up being my last day on earth. I pull my long black hair back into a ponytail to keep it out of the way. Who knows what I'm going to have to do today? I don't want any distractions.

As I look in the mirror, I'm yet again amazed I didn't figure out that I wasn't from both Mom and Dad. Dad taught me genetics long ago. Mom has beautiful blonde hair and blue eyes. Dad has sandy brown hair and blue eyes. There is no feasible way they could have made a black haired, green eyed daughter.

By the time I'm back in my room, Kallen has used his magic to make himself some new clothes. He looks great in jeans and a tight black t-shirt. He doesn't get as cold as I do. Lucky me, because I like the view. I walk over to him and wrap my arms around his waist, laying my cheek against his chest. His arms curl around me and he holds me for a few precious minutes.

He shifts back a little and kisses the top of my head. I look up at him and he says reluctantly, "I suppose we should join the rest of your family now."

Our respite is coming to an end all too soon for me, but he's right. "I guess we have to get back out there, huh?"

"It would be wise."

I groan. "Fine. You should kiss me first, though. Then at least I'll have something good to think about."

He doesn't need to be told twice. He closes the gap between us again and swoops down to give me a slow, gentle kiss. Releasing my lips reluctantly, he stands back with his hands on my shoulders. "I believe it is time we spoke with your grandmother about who we are up against. Knowing their strengths will help us determine their weaknesses."

"I hope so." With a heavy heart and mind, I open my bedroom door and mentally prepare myself to face the next couple of days without going insane. Or killing anyone. Or getting killed.

Boy, and I thought the tension was thick between Kallen and my parents this morning. The kitchen reeks with it now, like a tension skunk was attacked by a wolf and let loose its stench. We're going to have to scrub the walls with tomato juice to get it all out.

Mom looks miserable, and I'm pretty sure Dad still wants to punch Grandma in the face if the steely look in his eyes means anything. Grandma looks stoic but she seems to be unraveling some around the edges. I wonder what's been happening in here while Kallen and I took our little break. Actually, check that, I don't want to know.

I guess I'll just plunge right in. I don't think I can make it any worse. "Grandma, what can you tell us about the Witan?"

She looks relieved to be able to talk about something other than what they were talking about before we came in. "Quite a bit."

"Great." I pull out a chair and sit across from her at the kitchen table. Dad rises from the chair he was appearing to sit in so

Kallen can sit down as well. Dad moves to the corner of the room where he can observe and still glower at Grandma. She pretends not to notice.

"I'll start with his Derwydd. She's the King's advisor, and when the King is not available, she acts as judge and jury to Witches who have become too visible to the Cowans or have broken any other magical law."

I can't help rolling my eyes at the term. "Can't you just say humans? Saying 'Cowans' makes them sound lower than human. Until last week, I thought I was human, and my brother is still half human."

"Brother?" The shock on her face as her head swings to Mom is palpable. "You have a son?"

Oh, god. Mom and Dad must have been keeping that a secret. Kallen shoots me an 'are you insane' look. What did I just do? "Um, he was adopted," I try lamely but Grandma obviously knows the cat, or the brother, is out of the bag. I'll try diversion instead. "You were saying something about Grandpa's Derwydd?"

Grandma visibly shakes herself. "Yes, of course." Smart woman, she knows when to drop a subject. "Maeva is your grandfather's Derwydd. She is...intoxicating." Is that bitterness in her voice? Or jealousy? I wonder if Grandpa has a wandering eye. Or wandering other parts. Eew. Then again, they have supposedly lived apart for the last eighteen years. I would imagine Grandpa is free to have other women in his life. The thought of my sixty some year-old grandfather dating isn't a pleasant one and I grimace from the mental image.

"She is a seductress?" Kallen asks.

"Yes," Grandma says between tight lips.

Great. This is going to be another one of those conversations where I'm completely ignorant about everything we discuss. If Kallen mocks me, I swear I'm going to kick him under the table. "What's a Seductress?"

Kallen has a mocking gleam in his eye, despite the sober expression on his face, when he says, "She has the ability to seduce. She can persuade others to do her bidding by making it seem seductive."

I narrow my eyes. "You're just a walking dictionary, aren't you? Thanks for clearing that up for me."

"A Seductress is someone who can use her magic to persuade others to do things against their will – no matter how desperately they fight against her. She taps into a person's deepest desires," Mom explains.

No wonder Grandma doesn't like the woman. Who would want someone like that around her husband? "That sounds wrong. Why would Grandpa want someone like her around?" Other than the obvious reasons, I guess. Probably best not to say that out loud.

Grandma pulls herself together, but her jaw is still tight. "A Seductress is a powerful ally. Maeva settled many challenges to your Grandfather's throne without bloodshed. And when someone has broken one of our laws, a little time with Maeva will make them confess to everything and more easily comply with their sentencing."

"Let me guess, they're sentenced to death." Burning at the stake, probably.

Grandma looks shocked. "Good heavens, no! We're not barbarians. Their power is bound one to three times, depending on how powerful they are. Usually, their sentence is to live magic free and be imprisoned for an appropriate length of time. If the crime is severe enough, they remain incarcerated for their lifetime."

"So, the death penalty never comes into play?"

She shakes her head emphatically. "No." Her face starts to turn pink. Now she's getting it.

I lean back in my chair and cross my arms over my chest. "So, let me get this straight, then. Even though I have not committed any magical crimes, I have not used my magic to intentionally inflict harm on another Witch or human, and I saved this realm from the Fairies coming back to wreak revenge, I am still somehow evil enough to be put down like a dog." Turning to Kallen, I add, "It's a good thing I didn't hurt my leg up in the mountains, you would have had to shoot me to put me out of my misery."

"I probably would have tried splinting it first."

I nod appreciatively. "Very considerate of you. And you're not even a blood relative." I turn back to Grandma and she is beet red now. Good, she should be embarrassed about what her *kind,* as she likes to say, are trying to do to me.

"Of course it is wrong what your grandfather and his Witan want to do. That is why I'm here."

I'm about to say something else when I feel an icy cold hand on my shoulder. I look up at Dad. "I'm right there with you hating these..." I think he's trying really hard not to swear. "...Witches. But we need to find out as much as possible before they get here."

I slump a little in my chair. "Fine. So, how do you fight against a Seductress?" If Grandma and Grandpa have lived apart for eighteen years, I wonder again just how close Grandpa is to his Seductress advisor – and who's in charge of whom. I bet Grandma wonders that, too.

Kallen answers me. "You have to see her for what she really is. A Seductress's power is in her ability to make you see what your heart wants to see. If you favor thin blondes, then that's what she looks like to you. If you like rugged men, then that's what she looks like to you. She becomes one's physical dream. Once she has caught your interest, she wheedles her way into your mind and convinces you that you are living in a fantasy world with your dream lover and she can get you to do almost anything."

My brows come together as I ponder that. "Okay, but what if you're already with your dream lover?"

A small, smug smile touches Kallen's lips because he knows I'm talking about him. Great, just what he needed - another ego boost. "Then she will become that person; confusing you, so you don't know who is real and who is the illusion. She is a master of nuance and can easily discern from body language, speech, and facial expressions whether she is projecting cor- rectly. Any subtle change in how you respond, she picks up on it and alters her behavior until you are so confused you become clay in her hands."

"So, can't we just use Seductress magic against her?"

Mom shakes her head. "I'm so sorry I haven't taught you all of this. Each Witch has an affinity for a type of magic. We can all dabble in this or that, but we all have our specialties. Seduction is an extremely difficult magic to produce. If you don't have an affinity for it, it is almost impossible to perform."

Hmm, I wonder what my affinity is. Other than blowing things up. "If she's that good, then how do you fight against her?"

Grandma's lips form a grim line. "Most can't. That is why she's so powerful. It takes a strong talisman to shield you from Seductress magic."

"Okay, then how do I make a talisman like that?" Kallen raises his brows as a reminder of what happened the last time I tried to work a spell. It's going to be a long day.

"There is an ancient way, a way which requires a lot of power." Grandma looks pointedly at me.

I hope she knows I'm not a mind reader. "And that would be…" I prompt.

"It is similar to the Fairy trap your mother has set up outside."

"You know about that?"

She smiles slightly and inclines her head. "A Witch can most often feel the magic of another. I felt it as I passed through it. I didn't know specifically what it was meant to trap, but I reasoned that out." She glances quickly at Kallen and then back to me.

"Okay, how do I do this?"

"You use tree magic."

What am I, a druid? "What do you mean tree magic?"

"Interesting," Kallen says and he and Grandma lock eyes again. Secrets, secrets, secrets. I wonder if I could reach my leg far enough to kick them both under the table.

"What's so interesting?" I ask at the same time Mom says, "I've never heard of this before."

Grandma responds to Mom first. "Tree magic is for the most part a lost art with Witches."

A shadow touches her eyes and she looks away from Mom too quickly. Is she lying? I turn to see what Kallen is thinking of this, but he's still looking at Grandma as if she's about to grow another head or turn over another clue as to what her big secret is.

"Can Fairies do tree magic?"

Kallen drags his eyes to me. "No."

My brows come together in a scowl. He could have elaborated. "Do you know what tree magic is?"

"Yes."

"Do you think you could use multiple syllables?"

"No." This time he looks like he's just trying to annoy me, which he does successfully.

Ignoring him now, I turn back to Grandma. "How does it work?"

"In a forest such as this, the roots of the trees interlace themselves." She laces her fingers together as an example. "Where these roots touch each other, the trees share their energy with each other, working together to maintain equilibrium within the forest. It is possible to use this woven network to communicate a spell amongst the trees."

"So, it spreads like a virus?"

"That would be an apt description, yes."

I purse my lips as I think about how this would work. "How do you define which trees you want the spell to travel to?"

Grandma smiles as if I've just gotten an A on a test. "That can be tricky. Each tree must be precisely marked. If the circuit is not kept intact, the magic will escape its boundaries. That mustn't happen."

Ominous. "What happens if it does?"

"There are guardians of tree magic and we do not want to anger them. Nor harm their trees with magic."

Double ominous. "So, because our situation isn't dire enough, you want to teach the person who sets *air* on fire, a magic that involves trees." I'm not Smoky the Bear, but even I can figure out that fire and trees are not a good combination.

Grandma smiles again, but this time it's a sad smile. "You have it within you to perform this magic. I am confident."

"Glad you are," I mutter which makes Grandma's smile a little less sad. "What do I have to do?"

"Perhaps we should learn of the other Witan members before we begin to prepare," Kallen says. He's right, I'm being too impatient.

Grandma agrees. "There are six other members of the Witan. Three of them are the binders – Annika, Louhi and Midar."

"Do any of you have normal names? How am I supposed to remember all this?"

Kallen cocks his head to the side. "I did not realize Xandra was such a common name in this realm." Point taken. I give him a slightly nasty look and gesture for Grandma to continue.

"Witches take immense pride in their names, my dear. I'm afraid it has become a way to stand apart from the Cow...Humans."

I shake my head. Name pomposity, how inane. Wanting to

move this conversation along again, I ask, "Do the binders have different affinities?"

Grandma nods. "Yes, Louhi works Ekstasis magic. He has the ability when performing a binding to lift the Witch outside of him or herself."

"What do you mean?"

"He creates such inner excitement and ecstasy, the Witch's mind separates from the physical, such as in hypnosis. A person under hypnosis is easily controlled because the mind has been taken out of the equation."

"So, he creates vegetables?" Okay, that's extra scary.

Kallen looks honestly confused. "What do vegetables have to do with the power of Ekstasis?" I keep forgetting he's new around here.

"It's just a term we use here when things like a car accident happens and the person's body is still alive, but their mind is gone." He looks slightly less confused, but not much.

"That sounds like an apt description," Grandma says.

"Can the Witch get his or her mind back?"

"If Louhi allows it, yes."

That's really scary now. "So, he holds the Witch's mind hostage?"

Grandma nods. "In a way. He can sever the ties between the conscious mind and the body, and when he does so, only he can reverse the effects. This, of course, is limited to only those who have committed major offenses and are too dangerous to have out in the world."

"So, you give them a lobotomy." Dad says from his corner. That's sure what it sounds like to me, too.

Grandma's lips purse and she says, "It is similar, yes."

"And if this guy ever gets hit by a bus, all the Witches whose conscious minds he's holding hostage are just screwed, then."

Grandma sighs heavily. "Yes, that is correct."

Okay, I'm done hearing about this guy. "Who's next?"

"Midar is another binder. He has the ability to plant emotions in one's mind."

"I take it he doesn't plant good emotions." It sounds like he's starting a garden. I'll have a row of jealousy over there and here I think I'll plant some heartache.

Grandma's lips form a flat line for a moment. "He can. If he chooses."

"I'm guessing he doesn't choose to do that very often."

"No, not in his role with the Witan. In his private life, I suspect he may abuse his power."

"Huh? What do you mean?" And then it dawns on me. "Oh, do you mean to get women to like him or something like that?"

"Along those general lines, yes. But I have never had enough proof to bring before the other Witan members."

Grandma really doesn't seem to like these people. I'm starting to believe that the last eighteen years have been painful for her. "Okay, so stay away from Midar unless you want to feel suicidal or something equally as bad. Got it."

"The last binder is Annika. She is a practitioner of Sympathetic magic. She works with likenesses."

"Huh?" Okay, I keep repeating that but I'm not going to get this stuff through osmosis. It needs to be spelled out for me. I'm certain I just heard Kallen chuckle but when I look at him, his face is a blank page.

"She creates a likeness of the person she wants to control." Grandma thinks for a minute. "You may recognize it as a voodoo doll."

"Voodoo dolls are real?!" Scary. I could be a pin cushion in someone's hands right now.

"They are only real when a powerful Witch capable of working Sympathetic magic has created the 'doll.'"

"Do I even want to know what the last three can do?"

Grandma gives me a tired smile. "One must always know her enemies."

"Fine, lay it out for me. I'm guessing they can walk on water and control the elements."

She laughs softly. "Even the Witan are not that powerful."

"That's good to hear. So, what do they specialize in?"

"Two are the ones sent out after an errant Witch – Davina and Beren. Beren's affinity is scrying. He is capable of locating a Witch within a thousand miles simply by looking into a reflective surface."

"So, he's like a bloodhound? He can sniff out a Witch?"

Grandma's lips turn up at my description. "He could be compared to one, yes."

Must be another one on the Witan Grandma doesn't like. But then again, I don't get the impression she likes any of them. And then another thought hits. "If he's so good at this, why couldn't he find Mom?"

It's Mom's turn to smile. "Because a very powerful Witch taught me how to shield myself."

She and Grandma exchange a look. "Something that Witch deeply regretted when you couldn't be found." Too bad, Mom still looks proud of herself.

Wanting to get off this awkward topic, I ask, "What does the other one do?"

Grandma clears her throat. I think she might have a tear or two in her eyes. "The other is a Summoner. Once Davina has a location, she can work a summoning spell that will compel the prey to come to her."

"Does she have a thousand-mile range, too?"

Grandma shakes her head. "No. Once Beren has located their prey, they must travel within a hundred-mile range for Davina's summoning spell to work. She then compels him or her to follow her to where the Witan reside."

"She's a modern-day Pied Piper."

"I am not familiar with that reference," Kallen says.

I love it when he doesn't know something. "It's a children's story about what happens if you don't keep your word. Basically, a town hired the Pied Piper to get rid of rats that were running rampant. When he did by compelling them to drown themselves, the town refused to pay him. To get even, he compelled all the children except one to follow him away from the town and they were never heard from again."

"What happened to the one left behind?"

"He was pretty lonely after that."

Kallen's brow scrunches as if he's trying to figure out if I'm joking or not. I think I'm going to leave him hanging. "What does the last one do?"

Grandma is suddenly squirming in her chair as she gives furtive looks towards Mom. Mom's mouth is set in a firm line. Neither of them says anything. After several minutes of uncomfortable silence, I ask again, "What does the last one do?"

Mom speaks first. "Tell her, Mother."

Grandma sighs a great sigh of anguish and sorrow but still doesn't say anything. This waiting is killing me. I'm very much an instant gratification kind of person and this tense silence is driving me nuts. I look at Kallen for an answer, but he shrugs his shoulders letting me know he's just as ignorant as I am. "Will one of you please tell me?"

Mom finally gives me an answer. "Fatin is a master of Evocation and Exorcism."

"Exorcism? Like getting rid of ghosts?"

Grandma nods, but she still doesn't speak. Mom must answer me again. "Yes, Xandra, Evocation is the ability to call forth spirits in preparation for exorcism." She sighs. "Not all spirits who linger in this plane are good. Sometimes, a Witch will hold on because he or she wants to take revenge on an enemy or someone who they believed committed some wrong against them. Some will even try to take control of another Witch's body."

"But you don't do any of those things, so he'll leave you alone, right?" I sound naïve even to my own ears.

Kallen is looking at me with sympathy and he lays his hand on mine. "A threat to the ones you love may cause you to do things you shouldn't." He looks pointedly at me now. When we were fighting the other Fairies, they used my little brother to get me to do what they wanted. It just didn't work out as they planned.

"You think they'll threaten to exorcise Mom and Dad?"

With a meaningful look in the corner where Dad is, he says, "I think they will threaten at least one of your parents, yes."

"I'm the only non-magical one here. I would be the easiest target." Dad says this matter-of-factly, but his eyes belie his stoicism.

I'm mad now. They better not try to do anything to my parents. If they do, I won't care what imbalances I create. They'll pay ten times greater for any pain they cause my family.

Grandma sees the murderous look in my eyes. With steel in her own, she says, "There are protection spells which may be used against all the Witan's affinities, as well as spells that can render their spells null and void. We'll protect your family – whatever it takes."

This is this first time all day I believe Grandma. Dad is no longer the only one in the room turning into a sociopath. Grandma looks like she's going to bring eighteen years' worth of pain to each and every one of the Witan. Go Grandma. Maybe she and I will get to the cookie making, after all.

Dad speaks up from the corner again. "How long do you think we have before they arrive?"

"I would be surprised if they're not here by tomorrow morning."

"Do you really think they can prepare in such a brief period of time?" Mom asks. I think she was hoping Grandma would say next week, or even next year. Nope, they'll be here tomorrow.

"What do we do first?" I ask. I'm all wound up and I need to do something or I'm going to freak out.

Instead of answering me, Grandma focuses on Kallen. "Are you powerful enough to defend against any of these types of magic?"

Kallen is cool and confident as always. "Ekstasis will not work on a Fairy. The Fae are too in tune with their mind and body for them to be separated from each other. It is the difference between how we draw magic – filling ourselves with it as opposed to using it externally as Witches do."

I can't decide if he's slamming Witches or just speaking the facts. Guess it doesn't matter if he can provide some defense against the Witan. "Do you think I have that ability?"

Kallen looks thoughtful. "I would imagine that is the case. Your magic is internal. You command it from within as I do."

I'm going to go ahead and trust him on this one. "Okay, one down and six more to go." I turn to Grandma. "You said the tree magic will strip away Maeva's Seduction?"

She nods. "Yes, it will take away any illusions she is creating."

"What about the scryer? Why is he a danger to us? They already know where we are."

Mom answers this time. "If the scryer is using his magic, he can see not only where we are but what we are doing, as well. It's not just locations he sees."

Oh, that sucks. "So, we can't ambush them because he'll know what we're doing to prepare and find us if we're hiding?"

Mom nods. "Right. We won't have the advantage of surprise on our side."

Great, a living nanny cam. That should make things fun. "What about the Summoner?"

Kallen speaks up. "Fairies are also immune to Summoning spells meant for Witches."

"What about Summoning spells for Fairies?"

His mouth forms a hard line. "If the magic is still known, it would be effective."

"The magic is still known," Grandma says. "We need to shield from both Beren and Davina."

"How?"

"By creating an illusion, one they can't latch onto," Mom says and there's a gleam in her eyes.

I'm intrigued. "What do you mean?"

"One of my affinities is to create illusions," Mom says with a smug smile.

A smile also touches Grandma's lips as she remembers. "Yes, your mother could create an illusion that she was fast asleep in her bed while she was actually outside picking wildflowers or practicing her magic in the middle of the night."

Mom laughs at the memory. "At least it was all innocent fun."

Kallen leans forward. "Are you strong enough as a spirit to create an illusion that big?"

Mom is all confidence now. "Yes."

"How long can you hold this illusion?"

"My longest was two days. With my diminished power I can probably hold it at least twenty-four hours."

Kallen nods appreciatively. "What do you need from us?"

"I need an image of the five of us that I can hold in my mind. I think this image will do just fine." Mom grins. "Seeing us sitting around the kitchen table enjoying ourselves, not caring what they are doing should throw them off their game a bit."

"How will the illusion keep them from latching onto us?" I ask.

"Their magic is limited by having to have exact, what's the word? Coordinates. The illusion will function as a curtain they can't get past," Grandma explains.

Seems simple enough. Right. Because things like this go smoothly all the time. Not that I'd really know personally, but it never goes smoothly on television. Ugh. My head's starting to hurt. "Do you think we could take this one at a time? Maybe we could start with the tree magic or something and then work our way down the list."

Kallen raises his brows at my impatience but doesn't say anything. Mom looks sympathetic to my being antsy, but she turns to her mother for direction, which I don't like. I don't care how helpful Grandma's being. I really hate that this comes down to a woman who we still don't know exactly why she's here, or if she's one hundred percent on our side.

Grandma rises to her feet. "Alright, let's make the mighty oaks become our shield."

Chapter 7

Those of us with corporeal form put on some warm clothes to go out and play with trees. Too bad Zac's not here because he'd be in heaven. He loves being outside in the snow. I get another ping as I think about him. I hope he and Aunt Barb can come home soon.

Circling the house, Grandma walks ahead of us studying the trees. I have no idea what she's looking at, or what basis she's using to pick out which trees to use. What I do know is Kallen looks absolutely fascinated as he watches her with eagle eyes. "Why are you so excited?" I ask him.

Slipping my hand in his, he tries to look nonchalant. "I am always interested in learning about magic I am not familiar with."

I narrow my eyes at him. "Uh huh, why do I think you're not telling me the whole story?"

"I have no idea what you are talking about."

I'm about to say something else when Grandma stops short and we almost walk into her. "The trees here are marvelous," she says. "I would have loved to live among them." I don't think she's really talking to us. She seems to be musing out loud to herself.

Turning around to face us, she says, "There are enough oaks surrounding the house that we will be able to make a large circle of protection. Xandra, I need you to take this," she hands me a small bowl of stuff she mixed before we came outside. It's clay she brought with her in a glass jar and salt ground together until it turned into a paste. Then she added my blood. It was only a few drops, but maybe I should start taking some iron supplements if I'll be adding my blood to spells.

I take the bowl from her with its murky, grayish brown paste. It smells awful – whether from the blood or the clay, I'm not sure. I scrunch up my nose in distaste. "What am I supposed to do with it?"

"You will mark seven trees as you say the protection spell. Seven is the number that represents the dominion of the soul and mind over body. It will cast aside any attempts at altering our perception of reality and provide a sphere of protection for our bodies." Grandma walks to a particularly large oak and stops. "With your right index finger, you need to draw a circle on the bark with the clay potion."

With my nose still scrunched, I dip my index finger into the mix. It feels even worse than it smells. Trying hard not to inhale, I draw a large circle on the bark of the oak tree.

"Now, read the first part."

Grandma had written down the protection spell I need to speak. I read the part of the spell with a circle drawn next to it. *"From earth to heaven, I call to thee, Heavenly Divine, guardian of this tree. Circle of magic, circle of life, protect us now from mischief and strife. Forged images in malevolent aspect, our minds' eye will forcibly reject."* Who writes this stuff??

Grandma nods and starts walking to another oak about twenty feet away. "Draw the next symbol." She's all business now. Bossy, bossy. Has she been taking lessons from Kallen?

I look down at the page and copy the next image onto the tree. This clay stuff doesn't become less slimy and stinky with use. After I draw a t-shaped cross with a looped top, I read, *"By thou who whispers gentle yet strong, thou for whom my soul doth long, I beckon thee with magic old, let your Divine light, darkness unfold."*

The next tree, I draw equilateral triangles. At least, as equilateral as I can draw them on the bark of an oak tree using my finger. Grandma said this should invoke wisdom. I sure hope so. I could use some about now. *"By wood and wind, crimson and clay, your wisdom guides me this fateful day. Come to me, I beckon thee, from beyond the gates of death and birth, the one who gives all life upon earth. Guide me through this tangled path, of knowledge gained and wisdom's wrath."* Wisdom's wrath? I thought wisdom was supposed to be a good thing.

The next tree, I draw a chalice. Okay, my chalice looks a little bit like a sippy cup but, hey, I'm not an artist. *"The Divine chalice filled with love, water, salt and wing of dove, from your lips to mine, this elixir of life, hold me fast against nameless strife. Fill my body, cleanse my soul, wash away thine enemy's hold."*

I need to draw a candle on the next tree. I sure hope I'm not graded on the quality of my symbols. *"By wind and fire, this molten flow, brings light from dark in a hollow soul. Bless me now with your love, light and power, become one with me this fateful hour."*

Next is the shield. Or in my case, the almost circle with a couple of points on the top. *"Defender of sky, forest and field, breathe upon me your heavenly shield. Humbled by your mighty presence, fill me with your holy essence. With my life force held in hand, protect me as I make my stand."*

"This last tree will bind the spell and close the circuit," Grandma says as she moves to an elder tree.

"Shouldn't it be another oak?" I ask.

Grandma shakes her head. "The elder tree is a magical entity that has enough power to bind the oaks."

I look at the elder tree with more respect. I guess the term 'mighty oak' isn't as accurate as I thought. Looking down at my paper, I groan inwardly. I need to draw a pentacle and then place a drop of my blood on each point. Yeah, I need to take those iron supplements. I hope that won't affect Kallen when he kisses me since he's sensitive to iron.

Drawing the pentacle with the last of the clay mixture, I then take Mom's athame out of my pocket and jab the end of my finger. Squeezing a drop onto each point, I read the final part of the spell. Grandma called it the Act of Drawing Down the Moon. Mom was familiar with it, but not that its origins were this old. I read through it once in my mind before reading it out loud, making sure I say it precisely.

"Bewitching Goddess of the crossroads
Whose secrets are kept in the night,
You are half remembered, half forgotten
And are found in the shadows of the night.
From the misty hidden caverns
In ancient magic days,
Comes the truth once forbidden
Of thy heavenly veiled ways.
Cloaked in velvet darkness

A dancer in the flames
You who are called Diana, Hecate,
And many other names.
I call upon your wisdom
And beseech thee from this time,
To enter my expectant soul
That our essence shall combine.
I beckon thee O Ancient One

From far and distant shore,
Come, come be with me now
This I ask, and nothing more."

A gentle wind begins to blow through the forest, and it takes me a moment to realize it's following the circuit of the trees I marked. It picks up speed and soon loose snow is spiraling around us, marking the walls of the protection spell as it circles around the house. I'm assuming this means I did it right. If the proud smile on Grandma's face means anything, then I'm assuming correctly.

"Remarkable," Kallen whispers. Why is he so awestruck over this?

Narrowing my eyes, I say quietly enough so Grandma can't hear above the now whistling wind, "What, are you her number one fan, now?" Okay, that may have been a little testy of me, but it was only a few hours ago that he was just as leery of her as I am. If he's not going to tell me what changed his mind, then he must put up with me being grouchy about it.

Kallen says something but I don't hear him. The wind is whipping around the protection circle now and there's a loud piercing sound underneath it that makes me put my hands over my ears. I fall to my knees; the sound is raging in my head, deadening all my other senses. I wonder if this is how dogs feel when one of those high-pitched dog whistles are blown. Kallen is kneeling in front of me. He's saying something but I can't hear him. He looks worried and he doesn't look like he's bothered by the sound like I am. I wonder if he can even hear it. Maybe it's the Witch part of me that's being affected?

Grandma's in front of me now. She's kneeling in the snow in her skirt again. I wonder why she hasn't changed her clothes. She's pulling on my arms, trying to get me to uncover my ears. She's saying something but I can't hear her any better than I could hear Kallen. She turns to him and says something, and the next thing I know, Kallen is pulling my arms down. Why are they doing this to me? The sound is so painful now, it feels like it's piercing my brain, fileting it, and then shredding it to pieces. Kallen gets my hands away from my ears. He shrinks back slightly, I'm assuming from the death glare I know I'm giving him, but he holds my arms firm.

"Xandra!" Grandma shouts. "Accept it! Stop trying to block it. Let the magic take hold!" Let the magic take hold? Is she crazy? It's trying to kill me.

"Xandra, listen to her," Kallen shouts. I shake my head adamantly. I don't want to die like this. He puts his hands on my cheeks. "Trust me!" And then his lips are on mine.

I thought I was mad at him a second ago. Now I'm really angry. How dare he kiss me thinking it's going to make everything better? I'm not Snow White or Sleeping Beauty. In this world, a kiss doesn't solve everything. I put my hands on his chest to push him away so I can tell him exactly what I think of his egotistical, chauvinistic, Dark Ages, macho crap when I realize something. The sound isn't as deafening as it was a minute ago. It's quieting in my head. As my body begins to relax, Kallen's kiss becomes gentler and I feel myself responding. My kiss becomes hungry as the last bit of pain dies away. Now, all I feel is passion – and power. My body feels as if it's glowing from the inside out. This is different than using my Fairy magic. This is power that radiates from my pores, makes my skin tingle as my internal light shines through. I wind my arms around Kallen, pulling him closer. He hesitates for a heartbeat but then is swept away with my passion. He is mine. I have become the Seductress, the Huntress, Guardian of Mind and Body, Talisman of Peace and Safety, Defender of Light. The Wisdom that has filled me will lead us down the path of justice.

I feel the light become brighter within me as our lips dance in passion and love. With eyes closed, I see it stream forth, filling the circle created by the trees, shining its protection on everyone and everything inside of it. As the light swells to a climax, I am filled with a sense of divine peace that settles in my very core. That's the last thing I remember before my body collapses in Kallen's arms.

Chapter 8

It's always so disorienting to pass out one place and wake up in another. Not that I've passed out a lot, but it seems to be happening often lately. I'm lying on my bed and the blinds are closed, but I'm pretty sure it's getting dark out. I must have been out for a while. I turn my head and Kallen's face comes into view. He's lying on his stomach next to me, with his arms folded under his head. His eyes are closed, but as soon as he realizes I'm awake, he opens them.

"You were sleeping the sleep of the dead. I am glad to see you have returned to us."

I lift my arms over my head and stretch. For some reason, I'm sore all over. "Did I miss dinner? I'm starved."

His eyebrows rise in amusement. "You only missed it by several hours."

I frown. "What do you mean? It doesn't look that dark out yet. Why did you eat so early?"

Now he looks even more amused. "What time do you think it is?"

I cheat and glance quickly at the clock. "Five thirty."

He chuckles. "Good guess. AM or PM?"

No, he can't mean what I think he means. "PM," I say obstinately.

"Guess again. That is not the sun setting," he says as he points to the window. "That is the sun rising."

"What? Why did you let me sleep so long?" There's so much to do and they just let me lay in bed all day? Mom and Dad never let me do that. This seems like a strange time for them to start.

"It was not our choice. You proved to be a more powerful conduit for the spell than your grandmother thought you would be. You were unable to be roused as your body adjusted to the onslaught of magic racing between you and the protection circle."

I groan. "I can't believe I wasted an entire day being passed out. Is there ever going to be magic that I can do correctly?"

Kallen chuckles again. "The question is not 'can you do the magic correctly,' the question is, are you too powerful to perform certain spells without ramifications. Probably."

"Maybe I should just have you and Mom bind my powers again and call it good."

Kallen looks surprised. "Why would you willingly give up your magic?"

I shrug. "I haven't needed it the last seventeen years. What do I need it for now?"

He looks at me like I'm crazy. "Namely, to keep yourself alive."

"But if my powers are bound, no one would have to worry about me. I wouldn't be a threat to anyone."

Now he's looking at me like I have the naiveté of a two-year-old. "The simple fact that you exist at all is enough of a threat to scare even the most powerful Witch. No one would trust that you would allow your magic to remain bound."

"That sounds like a great future – constantly battling to stay alive. What if I let the Witan do it?"

His answer comes out as a growl. "I would sooner see you dead myself than let those monsters get their hands on you. If they bothered to keep you alive at all, they would keep you in a mindless stasis for the rest of your days. You would cease to be, either way."

That was intense. "Wow, tell me how you really feel about it."

His brows slam together. "I did…"

I put my hand up to stop him. "I was being facetious. I get that you really don't want me to have the Witan bind my powers. It's just a little overwhelming that there are always going to be people who want me dead."

He slips his arm out from under his head and uses it to pull me closer. "Then maybe you should spend more time thinking about people who very much want you alive."

That makes me smile even if it's not a solution. I kiss him lightly and then pull back. "Seriously, my life is always going to be one battle after another, isn't it?"

He takes several heartbeats to answer. I assume he's trying to decide between saying what I want to hear and speaking the truth. "Hopefully, once you have proven yourself stronger than the Witan, you will be left alone."

I can't help a strangled laugh. "Do things really work that way in the land of the Fae? Because they don't work that way here. In this realm, there's always someone who wants to prove they're stronger, meaner, or better than you. I might as well hang a sign on the door that says, 'challengers welcome.' It's dangerous for anyone to be around me."

He pushes a strand of my hair back behind my ear and then strokes my cheek with his thumb. "Your life may be difficult, yes. That does not mean you give up. You have a generous and courageous heart and you are surrounded by people who love you, me included. I will gladly take the danger you bring with you to keep you in my life."

I try to smile through the tears that have decided to well up in my eyes. "That's not fighting fair."

He looks honestly confused. "What do you mean?"

"You know you're irresistible when you're being so nice and sweet. You could probably convince me I can fly when you act like this."

His confusion morphs into a sexy grin. "I will keep that information safely tucked away for later. I can think of several things I would like to convince you to do with me."

I laugh. "I'm sure you can." I lean in and kiss him again. Just a sweet, gentle kiss, then I lean my forehead against his. "Can't we create a circle between realms and live there forever?"

"As much as I would like to have you all to myself like that, I am afraid you would miss your family."

"You miss your grandmother, right?"

Sadness touches his eyes. "Very much."

"Then why is it different for me? You chose to stay with me over going back to see her and your family again."

"I knew when I came here that I would never see her again. We said our goodbyes, and I know she is content to have me live here with you."

I sigh heavily. "I just wish life could be as simple as it was before I found out I had magic. It really hasn't done a lot of great things for me. Well, other than you I mean."

He strokes my cheek again. "That is a tragedy. You should be able to revel in the fact that you are a magical being."

"Maybe the reveling will come later. Right now, I'm pretty mired in the 'woe is me' aspect of knowing I have magic."

He's about to say something when there's a whisper through the door. "Kallen, is she awake?"

I groan. I'm not ready to face everyone yet. I'm sure they're all pretty disappointed in the fact that I just passed out on them. What are we going to do now that we're not even close to being prepared to face Grandpa and his Witches? "I'm awake, Mom. We'll be right out." Turning back to Kallen, I ask, "Are you sorry you stayed in this realm, yet?"

Instead of answering me, his lips meet mine and for several delicious moments, all I can think about is how good he makes me feel. Pulling back slowly after a last, lingering kiss, he says, "I would risk any amount of danger to be able to do that again and again."

I run my hand through his hair and pull him back to me for one more kiss. "Thank you for staying," I murmur against his lips before releasing him and forcing myself to sit up and get out of bed.

After a quick trip to the bathroom and running a brush through my hair and a toothbrush over my teeth, I go in search of my parents. They can be surprisingly hard to find sometimes, considering they can travel from room to room without using doors. They're masters at the game Hide & Seek. Zac and I always lose when we play with them.

Surprisingly, I find them outside. "What are you doing?"

Dad practically jumps out of his skin. At least, he would of if he had any. "Xandra, you about gave me a heart attack! I didn't hear you come out."

Ghosts can't have heart attacks. Or hearts. "Sorry, Dad. Why are you outside?"

Mom smiles sadly. "We're enjoying the peace and tranquility of the mountain." She doesn't have to add 'before it's ruined later today.'

"Where's Grandma?"

"She finally laid down a few hours ago. She was busy all night long getting things ready."

Color floods my face as I think about how I was sleeping instead of helping out. "I'm sorry I slept all day. I know you guys are probably really disappointed in me. I had meant to be more helpful."

Mom laughs. "Xandra, don't be ridiculous. Your body needed to recharge. The protection spell you worked is amazing and far bigger than your grandmother had thought possible. You've done plenty to help."

"It doesn't feel like it," I grumble but a little part of me is proud of myself. If the shield is that good, maybe there is a chance for everyone to survive. "Any news on when Grandpa should be here?"

Dad's face is grim. "He called your grandmother last night. He didn't know she was here, apparently, until he finally got it out of her assistant. She had the phone on speaker phone so we could all hear what he was saying."

"What did he say?"

Dad's eyes flash in anger. "He tried to convince her to see reason and to leave you here alone so 'what needs to be done could be done.' I wish I could get my hands on that man." Dad's sociopathic side is trying to come out again. I would hate to know what he would be doing right now if he still had a body. I don't think he'd be above going after Grandpa himself, which probably would get him killed. Again.

"What did she say?"

"I told him he would regret the day he tried to kill my granddaughter." Now it's my turn to jump out of my skin. It's so quiet out here in the snow; you'd think we'd hear each other moving around. I guess that's testament to how frazzled all our minds are. Probably not a good thing if we're going up against super stealthy Witches in the very near future.

Grandma has finally changed out of her pink wool skirt and is wearing brown pants and a pale-yellow sweater. Both are wrinkled as if she slept in them. "He will be here in just a few hours. He is coming ahead of the Witan, though I told him not to bother."

My brow furrows. "Why is he coming ahead of them?"

"He wants to convince your grandmother and me to give you up without a fight." Mom's the one who looks like a sociopath now. I am so glad all that anger is not directed at me.

"What, does he think we're just going to let him back in the house for a friendly little chat about whether or not you should let him kill me?" The disgust is oozing out of my mouth. There might be a little bit of fear there, as well. Not that he would be able to convince my mother, but I'm not betting the game on Grandma just yet.

Dad shrugs angrily. "Apparently."

A hand on my shoulder lets me know Kallen found us. "Perhaps we should go back inside and discuss how we are going to proceed."

Good suggestion. I hadn't put my jacket or anything warm on when coming outside and I'm starting to shiver. I lean into Kallen and walk back into the house with him.

"Are you hungry?" Grandma asks as she tries to suppress a yawn and walks ahead of us to the kitchen.

"Starved." I open the fridge to see what there is.

"Scoot," she says as she points me towards the table. "I'll make us some breakfast."

Mom smiles. "I remember waking up to your French toast. I missed your cooking over the years."

Did Dad just roll his eyes? Yet he gets so mad at me when I do that. I try to hide a smile, but he catches me and gives me a wink. I wonder what kind of strain having Grandma here is putting on his and Mom's relationship. They've always agreed on just about everything. I can't even remember the last time they were on opposite sides of the fence like this. Good thing ghost parents can't get divorced.

I sit down at the table next to Kallen. "Would anyone like to fill me in on all the things I missed while I was passed out?" If they couldn't wake me, I guess I was more unconscious than sleeping.

As Grandma clanks around the kitchen looking for everything she needs to make breakfast, Mom floats to the table. "Your grandmother made a number of talismans which will offer protection from certain spells. And Kallen worked an impressive circle that surrounds the house." Mom actually looks at him with respect. Wow, I did miss a lot.

"So, we're in a protection circle inside a protection circle?"

Mom nods. "Yes, and I've thrown up an illusion of us sitting around the table as an extra measure. It'll take an awful lot on their part to get through it all."

I notice she didn't say they *wouldn't* be able to get through it all. Where are the lies when I really need them? "But they will be able to get through?"

Mom pulls her bottom lip between her nearly invisible teeth. "I don't know."

Feeling dejected, I slump back in my chair wishing there was some way to know how this day is going to go. As if on cue, a feeling of being struck by lightning hits my body. It's a quick zap, probably only lasts a millisecond, but it's long enough for me to jump out of my chair and do an 'I just got struck by lightning dance.' "What the heck was that?" I practically scream as I look all over my clothes and stretch to check my backside to make sure I didn't really get struck by lightning. It takes me a second to realize the other four people in the room are looking at me as if I've just gone off the deep end. I look around at the puzzled faces. "Didn't anyone else feel it?"

With raised brows, Kallen says slowly, "Feel what, Xandra?"

Are you kidding me? I know I didn't imagine it. "Something just shocked me. Really hard. It felt like lightning." He looks doubtfully towards the window where the morning sun is starting to gleam off the snow. Okay, so there aren't many thunder and lightning storms in the middle of winter in Colorado. That doesn't change the fact that something just shocked me.

"Are you feeling alright, dear?" Grandma asks from where she is mixing eggs, milk, and vanilla in a bowl for French toast. "Perhaps you're still feeling the effects of the spell you performed yesterday?"

I grimace. Great, they all think I'm delusional. I slump back into my chair, trying hard not to pout. But as soon as I sit down, I feel it again. "What the hell?" I shout as I jump back up.

"Xandra!" Mom admonishes with a frown from where she's hovering by Grandma.

"Kallen, why don't you feel her forehead, see if she's feverish," Dad says as he hovers closer to me with concern all over his face.

I pull back from the hand Kallen is about to put on me. "I'm not sick. Something is shocking me!" Why won't they believe me? "Just because you guys can't feel it doesn't mean it's not happening."

Kallen still looks skeptical but asks, "What exactly does it feel like?"

I roll my eyes in exasperation. "I already told you. It feels like I'm being struck by lightning." As the last word leaves my mouth, another zap hits me. This time, I drop to my knees in pain as the zap lingers over my skin.

Kallen and Dad are by my side in a heartbeat. "Xandra?" Dad says but I hold up my hand in a plea to give me a minute and I close my eyes to breathe through the pain.

As soon as my eyes close, the pain is gone and I'm somewhere else. I'm in an airport somewhere and my breath catches in panic. Looking around me, I see a thin light extending through the crowd, like a glowing rope. It takes me a moment to realize the rope originates from me. I look down and see that it's part of me, extending out of the area around my navel. I can't see the other end through the crowd of people. Wow, is this from my tree spell? How cool is that!

In my head, I can faintly hear Dad and Kallen talking to me. I wish they would stop; I need to concentrate so I can figure out what's going on. With my hand, I bring my fingers and thumb together in a stop talking gesture and instantly their voices quiet. Finally. Now I can follow the light and see where it takes me.

I push through the crowd. Actually, the crowd seems to part for me even though they appear to not know I'm here. Finally, after getting past a heavy-set couple dragging their carry-ons and a screaming toddler, I see the end of the rope. It's wrapped around the head of a tall, skinny fortyish looking man with thinning brown hair and stooped shoulders. He's scowling and holding his temples as if he has a serious migraine. Good, I hope it hurts worse than the zaps I've been feeling.

As I walk closer to him, his pain seems to intensify. He's leaning forward now with his elbows on his knees. Sitting next to him is a willowy woman in a long, flowing blue dress who looks to be in her fifties with dull blond hair that's turning to gray and frown lines on her forehead. She has the oddest expression on her face – a combination of shock and determination. I watch curiously as the air around her shimmers a bit. Obviously, she's trying to work some magic. A satisfied smile appears on her face as I continue to walk closer. I'm not sure what she thinks she just did, but it must be good if that egotistical gleam in her eyes means anything. I just roll my eyes and shake my head which causes her to look down at herself. Her head snaps back up and she glares at me. I shrug like I don't really care what her problem is, because I don't, and I keep walking towards the man whose head is being squeezed by my bellybutton light.

It's his turn to drop to his knees now and a small mirror tumbles to the ground. I've reached him now and my shadow falling over him encourages him to open his eyes. "Who are you?" he demands gruffly.

He's pretty cocky considering he's the one in pain right now, not me. "I think a better question is - who are you?"

He glares at me, but he doesn't answer. Fortunately, I have a keen mind and I can use deductive logic as I look at the mirror that fell to the floor. A reflective surface. "Ah," I say as it hits me. "You must be Beren. Grandma told me about you."

Beren straightens but he doesn't rise to his feet. I can see the pain in his eyes still but he's trying to ignore it. Good for him. "You must be Xandra. You have saved us a trip to Colorado, thank you for that. Now, I order you to return with us to the King's home where you can be tried by the Witan and made to pay for your crimes against the magical world."

I don't think he expected me to start laughing because his eyes almost bug out of his head. "You really thought that was going to work?"

His brows slam together so fast and hard he winces in pain at the additional trauma to his already aching head. "I order you to return with us..."

I hold my hand up to stop him. "You seem to be under the impression that I am attached to you by this light thing." I gesture towards the beam of light that stretches from my navel to his head. I'm sure glad no one else can see it because it's rather disturbing. "But if I pull on it," I demonstrate by putting my hands on the rope of light that is surprisingly solid, "you will find that isn't the case." I yank on the rope and he falls forward onto his face. People walking by stop to stare at the man who just collapsed for no apparent reason. The woman next to him gasps. Oh, I almost forgot about her.

I look over at her appraisingly. I'm certain I know who she is now. "Maeva, right?"

Her smile is pure acid. "My reputation must have preceded me."

I shake my head. "No, you just seem way too into yourself to be anyone else on the Witan." Turning back to Beren, I pull on the rope again and he barely stifles a yelp. "Now, I just came to tell you that if you try scrying for me again, I'm going to come back a lot angrier than I am right now. And you really won't like that." Turning my eyes back to Maeva, I let them roam up and down her frame. "Sorry, you're definitely not my idea of a dream lover." With a simpering smile, I mentally retract the rope of light and walk back into the crowd.

Slowly, I feel myself coming back to the kitchen. I open my eyes to Grandma shaking my shoulders. Dad and Kallen have moved back, and Kallen looks mad. Now what did I do?

"Xandra, dear, are you with us?" Grandma's still shaking my shoulders, and now that I'm back in my own little reality, it's getting annoying.

"Yes," I say as I gently push her hands away.

"Thank goodness," she says with a sigh of relief. Looking over at Dad and Kallen, she says, "Do you think you could give them their voices back now?"

Sheepishly, I look up at the two of them. That's why Kallen is so mad. I've done this to him before when I wanted him to stop talking. With a small smile that hopefully contains the appropriate amount of apology, I take back the magic I used to make them both mute.

"Thank you," Kallen says dryly.

"Xandra? What happened?" Mom asks. She's hovering behind Grandma wringing her hands.

"I just met Beren and Maeva," I say as I get unsteadily to my feet. Grandma grabs my elbow and helps steer me back to the chair I was sitting in a few minutes ago.

"What do you mean, you just met them?" Kallen asks. At least he doesn't look mad anymore. Instead, his vibrant green eyes fill with concern.

"I mean, I just met them. We introduced ourselves, I told Beren to quit scrying for me and I told Maeva she isn't my type."

Grandma covers her mouth to hide the pure glee in her smile. "Did you really?" she asks. I nod and her smile gets bigger.

Mom is significantly less amused. "How is this possible, Mother?"

Grandma shrugs as she steps back away from the table and returns to put bread in the French toast batter and transfer it to the griddle. "As we discussed yesterday, she seems to have a strong connection to the protection circle and the trees. I cannot account for it, but she is more in tune with them than I had ever dreamed possible." There's a hint of worry in her eyes. She ducks her head and busies herself with flipping the bread on the griddle over hoping we don't see it. There's that secret of hers rearing its ugly head again.

"Tell us what happened," Dad demands gently. "You were physically here but your mind was gone for several minutes." He looks pointedly at Grandma before adding, "I don't like this."

"I'm fine, Dad." I'm not sticking up for Grandma, I'm just telling the truth. I am fine. And, there's no annoying lightning strikes hitting my body anymore.

"Where did you come upon them?" Kallen asks.

"They were in an airport. Apparently, they're on their way."

I look over at Grandma who is fuming now. She slams the spatula she just used to take French toast off the griddle onto the counter. "I knew he was lying to me."

I can't help but feel badly for her. The betrayal is too raw on her face. "I didn't actually see Grandpa there. Only Beren and Maeva," I say but the flashing behind her eyes tells me she doesn't care if I saw him or not. She still believes he lied to her about coming ahead of the others. I'm not sure why it matters so much, though. It's not like he was coming to kiss and make up. He was just hoping to be able to kill me sooner and easier.

Baffled, Dad says, "I don't understand how you intercepted them at an airport. You were right here the whole time." I'm not the only one new to all this crazy magic stuff.

"I think the protection spell brought me – or my spirit, or something – there. It was Beren trying to scry for me that was causing the shocks, I think, and the spell brought me to him. Only Maeva and he could see me." I explain about the rope of light coming from my navel stretching to Beren. Kallen looks at me dubiously but Grandma gasps. All eight of our eyes focus on her instantly.

"Mother?" Mom prompts.

Grandma is suddenly busy again with breakfast. "I had no idea there would be such a strong connection. Xandra must be immensely powerful."

"Is there something you're not telling us, Athear?" Dad asks.

Grandma looks up at him and quickly back down at the griddle.

BONNIE LAMER

"Don't be silly. What would I be keeping from you?"

A retort is on Dad's lips when the phone rings. Closing his mouth in a grim line, he floats to the voice activated phone and says, "Answer," followed by, "Hello."

"Where is Athear?" an angry voice demands through the speaker phone. "What has that horrible daughter of yours done to her?" Ah, the loving voice of my grandfather. I might make cookies with Grandma someday, but I'm quite sure the fishing with Grandpa is a definite no go.

Grandma shakes her head in disgust even though Grandpa can't see her. "Sveargith, quit being foolish. Your granddaughter has done nothing to me except welcome me into her home." Well, I sort of did.

"Beren called me from the airport. He said he can't scry for you – all he gets is a blank wall when he tries. He also said that girl showed up."

That girl? He won't even call me by name? I guess he's going with the theory that if he doesn't personalize me, it'll be easier when the time comes to kill me. Or maybe it's the whole saying a Fairy's name thing. I don't really care which it is. Either way, he's still an idiot.

Smugness plasters itself on Grandma's face and echoes in her voice. "How wonderful to hear the spell worked so well. You should be immensely proud of your granddaughter for being able to wield such powerful magic at such a young age!"

Grandpa's voice comes through as a growl now. "Proud of her? She almost killed Beren when she came to him and Maeva."

"Wow, is that your lie or theirs?" I ask, dumbfounded that things got blown so out of proportion. "I didn't even touch him." Okay, my belly button light did, but still.

"The only lies being told, young lady, are yours."

I turn to Dad. "I know I'm supposed to respect my elders, but would you mind terribly if I told Grandpa to go suck a rotten egg?"

Dad shakes his head. "Nope, you go right ahead. Why don't you tell him that for me, as well?"

"Of all the impertinence! Do you know who you're talking to, young man?" Young man? I've never heard my father referred to as 'young man' before. Though, I suppose Grandpa is pretty old.

"Sveargith, I believe you've lost all hope of having anyone here garner any respect for you," Grandma tells him.

Grandpa's quiet for a moment. Finally, with more pleading in his voice than he probably meant for there to be, he says, "At- hear, please, you have to understand. You know why this has to be done."

"Hang up," Grandma tells the phone and then Grandpa's gone.

Chapter 9

The next hour is spent eating breakfast, during which Mom and Grandma spend the entire meal reminiscing, much to the chagrin of Dad, and then they show me the talismans and amulets Grandma made the night before. Apparently, they're the standard stuff – Witch bottle repellents, see beyond the magical disguise necklaces, etc. Honestly, I stopped listening after the tenth or eleventh one. Yes, I probably should be paying attention, but my mind can't seem to concentrate on the details. I feel on edge, understandably I'm sure, and feel as if I could practically crawl out of my skin.

After half an hour of continuous fidgeting on my part, Mom finally asks, "Xandra, what on earth is wrong with you? You aren't listening to a thing we're saying."

"I am too," I say defensively pointing to what's in her hand. "You just said that's a Witch's ladder like the bracelet you gave me before. If you untie the knots, you let loose the magic."

"That was five amulets ago," she says holding up a necklace on a leather string that clearly has no knots in it. "This one prevents love spells."

I scrunch up my nose. "Love spells? Why would we need those?"

There's a hard glint in Grandma's eyes when she answers. "Because Maeva is not above using something so underhanded. Not to mention Midar."

"One of them might try to make me fall in love with them?" Eew. "I think I can fight that off without an amulet."

Kallen's sitting on the kitchen counter observing us. "Just think about me if you get hit with one of those. No one else will seem attractive to you," he says with a wink. Color rushes to my cheeks, even if he is only teasing, but I can't help a small smile either. Mom rolls her eyes, but I catch the corners of her mouth trying to move upwards as well.

Dad happens to be floating by during the exchange. He just came in from doing what he and Kallen call a 'perimeter check.' Dad watches too much TV. I don't know what Kallen's excuse is. "Same goes for you," Dad says as he swoops down and gives Mom a kiss on her pale check. A full-fledged smile breaks out on her face now.

Hmm. I wonder if Kallen and I would still like each other if we ended up as spirits. I hope we don't have to find out any time soon. Looking up at him, I say, "What if I'm not the target of the love spell, you are?"

He shakes his head. "Can't happen. A Witch can't make a Fairy fall in love with her with magic."

I narrow my eyes in doubt. Turning to Grandma, I ask, "Is that true?"

"In a way. You need to have some aspect of the person who is the target of the spell. A piece of hair, something. Since none of these Witches has ever met Kallen, they wouldn't have anything to draw on. And it is exceedingly difficult to work a love spell on a Fairy."

"But I've never met them, either. How could they do a spell on me?"

Grandma's lips purse together for a moment before she answers. Finally, she says, "Because your grandfather may have retrieved something while he was here. It only takes one hair to work a love spell, not to mention many other spells. He could have taken some from a hairbrush, or even gotten some on his clothes while he was in the house with you."

My jaw drops open as I turn to Mom. "He's that sneaky? I thought he originally came here to help?"

Mom looks embarrassed. "I'm not sure. My father is a much different man than I remember. He may have had ulterior motives."

I shake my head in disbelief. "And they're worried about me? They're the ones who are freaky and out of control." Right on cue, I feel a zap. This is getting old fast. I close my eyes and there's that belly button light again.

This time, I'm outside my house near the first oak tree I marked. Standing about fifteen feet in front of me is my grandfather. He's standing next to the car he parked on the side of the mountain road, probably because the protection spell wouldn't let him get closer. He's around six feet tall with a thick head of gray hair, and he's dressed in a tan overcoat over black dress pants and shoes that are so brightly shined, they reflect the light off the snow.

I don't know which one of us is more shocked. I guess the upside is he didn't lie to Grandma about coming ahead of the others. He just got here sooner than she expected.

Grandpa looks at the rope of light entwined around his hands and then looks back up at me. I think it's hurting him, but I can't tell for sure. He has a really good poker face. "What is this? How are you doing it?"

A laugh of disbelief escapes me. "You expect me to tell you so you*-99+ can try to counteract it. I may be young, but I'm not that naïve." Okay, I don't really know how I'm doing it, but even if I did, I wouldn't tell him. Just to add a little salt to his bad mood, I say smugly, "Grandma taught me how to do it." Sort of.

Wow, his face is turning red and I can see his teeth grinding together. I wonder if he's angrier at me or at Grandma for helping me. I guess it doesn't really matter—he's mad. I get it. His skin can't seem to decide if it wants to turn red from anger or green from the idea that his wife is working against him. It's a mottled brownish color now. "What have you done to my wife?"

I roll my eyes. I don't know how much more of this drama I can stand. I've never had drama in my life before. "Grandma's fine."

He points a shaky finger at me. "If you hurt her..." he threatens. It's hard to look intimidating with a rope of light around your hands that extends from someone's belly button, though.

I sigh heavily. "You know, if you would have taken half a minute to get to know me, you'd have figured out that I don't want to hurt anybody."

His whole body is shaking now as he shouts, "You opened the gateway between realms!"

"Yeah, to throw a couple of Fairies back through it. I didn't let any out!" I shout back.

"Then that wasn't a Fairy you brought home with you?"

"He's my boyfriend! He's not here to hurt anybody."

"All Fairies are evil, treacherous beings. None of them can be trusted."

"Yeah? It seems to me that except for my mother who renounced your ways, all Witches are evil, *murderous*, and treacherous. That's from my own *personal* experience. How many Fairies have you personally met?"

Grandpa is speechless for a moment as my words sink in. Finally, he blusters, "Witches are noble and..."

I cut him off. "You can say whatever you want, but do you honestly think I care what a man who tried to kill me – twice – has to say? How can you possibly be a representative of how good and noble Witches are when you want to kill your own flesh and blood? My God, you're a walking Shakespearian Tragedy."

His face turns beet red now, but he says more calmly, "The prophecy says..."

"Yeah, yeah. I know the prophecy: *A Witch's child of Fae is born when spirits of the realms are torn. Into the world destruction she brings while children cry and Angels sing. None may survive the vengeance of she, and immortal her soul is to be, to remedy the world of its natural discord*, blah blah blah," I recite from memory. Kallen told me about the prophecy when we were in the mountains. It's why everyone is so afraid of me. "So? Maybe it's you who brings the discord that forces me to destroy the world, did you think of that? Maybe it's a self-fulfilling prophecy."

I think I might have stumped him. He opens his mouth several times to say something, but no sound comes out. I've had it with him, and I throw my hands up in the air. "I'm going back inside. You can stay out here in the cold and figure out what you want to say to me. Just give me a shout when you have it all worked out." I'm not actually cold because my body isn't really here; I'm just making a point.

I think about the rope light retracting back to me and it does, just like it did at the airport. This time I don't yank on it, though, so Grandpa doesn't fall down and have more reason to be furious. Although, thinking about Grandpa flat on his face makes me chuckle. I would get great satisfaction out of seeing that. It's amazing how petty you can become when the world is out to get you. Well, *worlds* in my case. High road, I must take the high road, is becoming my mantra. Or as Mom would say, 'live and let live, fairly take and fairly give.' Ignoring Grandpa now, I close my eyes, preparing to bring my mind back to my body.

"I melt this wax as I melt your will. Child of darkness, your body be still. I bind these hands as I bind thee, a force unbreakable ties you to me. Sprung from seeds I've sown, your will is my own. Cast aside your desires, consumed by my fire, as I control your mind and bring justice to our time. As I beckon, come to me, your will is no longer free."

My eyes open back up and I glare at Grandpa as I slowly start walking towards him. A shadow of fear is in his eyes, but as I get closer, it's replaced with smug satisfaction. Looking at the small likeness of me he's holding a lighter against, I say, "I see Annika has been busy. Did you steal a picture from our house while you were there?" He doesn't answer me, but he looks guilty, so I'm certain that's what happened.

Squaring his shoulders, which causes the buttons of his overcoat to strain over his expanding waistline, he says, "It pays to take precautions."

"So, stealing as well as murder is okay. Wow, if those are the morals Mom grew up with, I'm surprised she didn't turn out to be a homicidal kleptomaniac. Oh, but that's right, she ran away from you and your morals."

His eyes flash with anger, but he holds his tongue in check, satisfied that I'm under his control now. Finally, I've breeched the fifteen-foot gap between us and I'm directly in front of him. He walks to the passenger side door of his car, opens it, and says, "Get in."

"No."

"I command you to get in the car," he practically barks.

"No."

Now he's really mad. "Your will is mine! You will do as I say!"

I can't help but laugh. I reach out and snatch the likeness from his hands. "My will is nobody's but my own. Now, as I said before, you can stay out here in the snow, but I'm going back inside." I close my eyes on Grandpa's wide eyed, open mouthed shock and bring myself back to the kitchen.

A gasp causes me to open my eyes quickly. I look up to see everyone staring at my hand, which now holds, in my opinion, a pretty poor wax likeness of me.

Chapter 10

"**W**here on earth did you get that?" Mom asks.

"From Grandpa. It's a little present from Annika. She did a crappy job though. I don't think it looks anything like me."

"It is much prettier than you are," Kallen teases and I throw the doll at him which he catches easily with one hand and laughs.

Ignoring him and turning my attention back to Mom and Grandma, I explain. "He stole a picture of me while he was here. Grandma was right; he is a sneaky old man."

Grandma raises her eyebrows. "I do not remember saying he was old."

A little color rushes to my cheeks. I guess she would be around the same age as him. "Anyway, he's outside."

Now, they're all shocked again. "He's here? Now?" Dad asks looking furious.

I nod. "Yup, he's down the road a little bit. I'm thinking he can sense the protection spell. He's probably trying to figure out how to get around it."

"You spoke with him?" Kallen asks looking up from his study of the likeness.

"Yeah. He tried to 'bend my will' to him using that thing." I make quotations with my fingers.

He smiles proudly at me. "Obviously, with no success."

"Do I get a gold star?" I tease.

"Perhaps," he says with a promise in his voice that tells me he's thinking more of kissing me than giving me a gold star. My cheeks turn pink again. Oh, if only we could be alone right now.

"I have a few things I'd like to say to the man myself," Dad growls and heads towards the front of the house.

"Jim, no, you can't," Mom says and quickly follows him. I can hear them arguing in hushed voices in the living room. I can't remember the last time I heard them argue. I hate what this is doing to all of us.

The phone rings, bringing my parents back into the room. They both still look angry, but they don't want to miss this phone call. There's really no doubt in anyone's mind as to who it must be. "Answer," Dad snarls at the phone. "What do you want, Sveargith?"

"Jim?" a feminine voice says in confusion.

Relief washes over Dad's face. It's my Aunt Barb. "Barb, sorry, I thought you were someone else."

"I'm glad I'm not, because you seem awfully upset with who-ever you thought it was going to be. I just wanted to check in. Is Xandra okay?"

"Hi, Aunt Barb. I'm fine." I can imagine her sitting at the kitchen table of the apartment she has in Denver for when she needs to stay over for work. Staying there now is for their personal

BLOOD PROPHECY

safety. I hate what magic is doing to our family. Though, my brother is probably in the other room oblivious and glued to a video game.

"Oh, honey, it's so good to hear your voice! How did things go with that awful young man?"

Dad can't hold back a snicker and Mom covers her mouth to hide her smile. Kallen looks at me with raised brows, almost like a challenge to say something derogatory. "Um, turns out he wasn't so bad," I say and Kallen's eyebrows are practically at his hair line now. "Actually, I kind of like him." I'm stammering. Between Mom and Dad and Kallen, I can't really concentrate on what I'm saying.

"You do? Well, I guess that's not too surprising. He was a handsome young man."

"Uh, Aunt Barb, he's right here."

"Oh, Xandra! Why didn't you tell me that?" She's obviously embarrassed now. It's Kallen's turn to snicker.

How was I supposed to know she was going to talk about his looks? "Sorry, Aunt Barb. Things are a little crazy around here with Grandpa wanting to kill me and all."

"What?! Jim, Julienne, what's going on there? Is she serious? I thought Fairies were after her."

"She took care of them," Mom says sadly, "and then my father decided he didn't like the amount of power she has."

You can almost hear Aunt Barb shake her head. "Unbelievable. You know, I'm still having a tough time with all this magic stuff. But your son is here chomping at the bit, ready to get home and in the middle of it all. I take it you want me to stay put with Zac here in Denver?"

120

"Yes," Dad says firmly. "The farther away from all this you two are the better."

"Alright. Keep us posted."

"Of course, give Zac my love," Mom says as they ring off. I bet if she could shed ghost tears, there would be some falling down her cheeks. She looks so sad it about breaks my heart. She must wonder if she's ever going to see them again. Yeah, me too.

The teasing atmosphere from a few minutes ago is gone as Aunt Barb's phone call dragged to the front of all our minds what we're facing and what's at stake. I need to change the subject. "Grandma, is it the tree spell or me being a Witch Fairy that's making it so that their magic isn't working on me?"

She looks thoughtful for a moment. "Honestly, I don't know. I would suspect the protection spell is doing most of it, but you are a powerful being. You may have some natural defenses against their magic."

I hope so because these people are determined. The phone rings before I can say that out loud. We all look at each other. It must be Grandpa this time and nobody wants to answer, so we're all riveted to our spots with our mouths closed.

After five rings, Dad finally says, "Answer."

"Athear, are you there?"

A sigh of pure disgust leaves Grandma. I don't think she's going to answer him. So, I do. "She's here but she doesn't want to talk to you."

"I demand she come to phone so I can be sure you haven't harmed her."

"You aren't in a position to *demand* anything." Dad is really fuming now. Good thing he's not able to wield sharp objects anymore.

"Oh, for heaven's sake, Sveargith, I'm right here," Grandma huffs.

"Are you alright?"

"Better than I've been in eighteen years." Ouch, that's gotta make Grandpa feel pretty low.

"I've tried everything in my power to make you happy these last years, even when I finally admitted to myself that staying out of your life was what you really wanted. But I still care about you and I'm worried for your safety."

Grandma narrows her eyes at the phone even though Grandpa can't see her. "I'm sure you've had plenty of company to keep you from worrying too much about me."

Grandpa's reply is indignant. "I have been faithful to you for forty years." Yeah, Grandma looks like she believes that one. With a Seductress as an advisor? Again, even I'm not that naïve. And again, eew, to the Grandpa dating image. Especially since I've seen Maeva, Grandma's way prettier.

By the looks on everyone's faces, we've all heard enough of this conversation to make us feel mighty uncomfortable. Kallen is the first one to say so. "Perhaps this is a conversation best had in private."

Grandma blushes but says towards the phone, "He's right. This is not the time or place for this conversation. We've had it a thousand times already. Unless you are willing to come to a peaceful understanding, there is nothing left to say."

"Please remember, Athear. You forced my hand." Grandpa utters an oath and hangs up, leaving us in an awkward silence.

"Um, what do you think he meant by that?" I ask but I'm not sure I genuinely want to know.

Grandma shakes her head wearily. "I don't know. Your grandfather is a skilled Witch; it would be difficult to guess what he will try."

"Is he skilled enough to get through the protection circles?"

I see the word 'no' forming on Grandma's lips but they're moving in slow motion as the walls of the kitchen start sliding forward. It seems to take my mind forever to figure out it's not the walls that are moving, it's me. I'm travelling backwards as my chair falls to the floor and a searing pain bursts from my abdomen, spreading like wildfire to the very tips of my fingers and toes. Kallen has jumped down from the counter with a look of panic on his face as he reaches out for me, but he's not quick enough, and I feel my head and back smack hard against the far wall, and the sickening metallic taste at the back of my throat must be blood.

Grandma and Mom rush from the room as Kallen drops to his knees next to me. Dad is looking at me over his shoulder, and he becomes a shade paler as I feel blood slide over my bottom lip and onto my chin. Even amongst the pain, it strikes me as odd that the sight of blood would bother Dad. He was a doctor, after all. Unless it's the fact that it's my blood that bothers him.

"Xandra, what happened?" Kallen's asking me as the room, sound and time suddenly start moving in synchronization again which overloads my senses even more.

"I don't...know," I say the best I can around a mouth full of blood.

Grandma's back now and she kneels in front of me and begins

123

putting that awful clay stuff on my forehead. I can't smell it this time because my nose and mouth are full of blood. I'm afraid to close my eyes, even though they're burning from strain, the pain might consume my soul if I do.

"Xandra, you have to repeat after me – '*I am your chalice, you are my shield, Divine power only you wield, please take from me the pain I feel, with Divine mercy my fate you seal.*'"

Somehow, I manage to get the words past my lips as I try to swallow back the blood. As the last words leave me, the pain intensifies to a crescendo and a blinding light encompasses me, forcing my eyes to close against my will. I let out a piercing scream and then it's gone. The pain is gone. The light is gone. I'm sitting on the floor of the kitchen with Kallen looking frightened, which I've never seen before, and Grandma looking relieved.

That is, until Kallen turns to her with fury in his eyes. "What just happened to her? What have you done?"

Grandma's skin flushes as she sits face to face with one of the most powerful Fairies alive, all his anger directed towards her. "I have never seen a bond like this before. She is *physically* connected to the protection circle."

"What does that mean?" Kallen demands. As I'm lying against the wall reveling in being pain free, he's getting ready to choke my grandmother. I can see his hands twitching, ready to strike.

"I think it means she was just hit by a car," Mom says quietly from the doorway and all eyes zoom to her.

Dad looks seriously confused. "Julienne, what are you talking about?"

"My father drove his car into the protection circle. If Xandra is physically attached to the spell, then it's as if she was hit by his car." Hmm, that would explain the blood. And the pain. Grandpa's a real ass.

Grandma gasps and puts her hand over her mouth. "No," she whispers. Mostly to herself, I think. "He wouldn't."

"Was that your plan, Athear? Connect my daughter to this spell so your husband could kill her easier?" I've never heard Dad shout before. I'm amazed at how much anger and hatred he can put into his words. I want my old, carefree dad back.

Grandma shakes her head as she pulls her hand from her mouth. "I swear to you, this is a mistake. I didn't know she'd become so ensconced in the spell. This is unprecedented."

"How do we fix it?" Kallen snarls and I reach out to take his hand before he can accost Grandma. She is the only person who knows how this works, after all.

"I-I don't know." Grandma looks so lost that my heart goes out to her.

Dad and Kallen have no sympathy for her. Dad has a finger pointed in her face, and she backs up an inch or two so his cold hand doesn't touch her skin. "You're a liar! Fix this, or so help me, I will spend the rest of my time on this plane making your life as miserable as you're making my daughter's."

"Dad, I think she's telling the truth." I push back and slide up the wall until I'm standing. Kallen grabs my elbow to make sure I'm steady on my feet. I'm okay, but I probably shouldn't make any sudden moves.

"Xandra, she had to have known," Kallen starts to say but I cut him off.

"No, she didn't." Even Grandma's looking at me in surprise.

"How do you know that?" Dad demands.

I think that's the harshest tone of voice he's ever used with me and I'm a bit taken aback. It takes me a second to find my voice again. "I just know, Dad. She's telling the truth."

Wow, did those words come out of my mouth? But as I think about it, I know it's true. Even if Dad and Kallen are both looking at me like a demon just burst forth from my head. The good news is, I think I stunned them both into silence. Turning to Grandma, I say, "Grandpa must know I'm connected to the spell. How could he have figured that out? Have you told him about this magic?"

She shakes her head. "No. I've never said a word to him."

I'm about to ask her if she's sure when I figure it out myself. "It's the light rope."

Kallen's brows are tightly scrunched. "Light rope? What do you mean?"

I roll my eyes at him. "Remember when I got pulled to the airport, I said there was a rope of light coming from my belly button. It was there when I met up with Grandpa, too. He must have figured it out."

"Son of a…"

"Jim," Mom admonishes before Dad has a chance to finish his thought.

Clearing his throat, he tries again. "So, the bastard knows he can hurt Xandra physically. How do we stop him from doing that?"

There's a determined glint in Mom's eyes. "Mother and I will take care of it. Kallen, why don't you help Xandra to her room?

She's been through a lot this morning, and she could probably use a little rest. I'm going to go introduce my father to some of the security precautions I've spread around the house and mountain over the years."

Her mouth set in a resolute line, Mom floats towards the front of the house with Grandma at her heels. I suspect Grandpa's going to wish he never got on the plane this morning.

"Your mother is right, you should go lie down," Dad says, concern replacing the anger in his voice from a couple of minutes ago. "I'm going to go with your mother."

"That may not be wise," Kallen warns.

"Probably not, but I'm not going to let Julienne face that man alone."

Kallen inclines his head in understanding. "Neither would I."

"Shouldn't I go out there as well?" I'm feeling like a big lump of 'not very helpful' right now.

"No, until we figure out how to separate you physically from the spell, we need to keep you better protected."

Frustration washes through me, but I know he's right. "Fine, I'll be in the bathroom brushing my teeth." Yes, I sound a little pouty, but I do need to brush my teeth. The bleeding may have stopped, but my mouth still tastes like blood. I push away from the wall and I'm surprised that I'm so steady on my feet. Kallen offers his hand but I shake my head and walk past him, leaving him and Dad in the kitchen staring after me. Okay, maybe I'm taking my frustration out on them, but I can't seem to help it.

I take my time brushing my teeth, trying hard not to think about how close I came to death. Tears are doing their best impersonation of Olympic swimmers trying to free themselves from my eyes, but I refuse to let them go. This would be an easy time to fall into a vat of self-pity, but I won't give in to it. So what if most of my biological family wants me dead, that doesn't mean I have to roll over and give them what they want. But it's sure easy to anchor my mind on the fact that most other seventeen-year-old girls aren't recovering from their grand-father trying to kill them.

Disgusted by all this feeling sorry for myself, I put my tooth-brush back in the medicine cabinet and slam it closed. Enough. Life took a crappy turn and I need to deal with it. Kallen's right, I should revel in the fact that I'm a magical being. I'm proud of who I am and I'm going to fight to stay alive.

I square my shoulders as I walk out of the bathroom and into my bedroom to change clothes. My shirt and jeans have blood on them. As soon as I walk through the door, hands grab my shoul-ders and push me gently against the wall. Kallen leans his fore-head on mine. "Do not ever scare me like that again," he says, and I can see a shadow of the pain he felt when he thought I was dying still lingering in his eyes.

I bring my hand up to his cheek and smile. "I'll do my best."

"I love you," he says as his lips capture mine in a long, sensual kiss. When ours lips part, he leans his forehead on mine again. "I have never said that to anyone before, you know."

That makes my heart spring to life. "I love you, too. And I've never said that to anyone before, either."

He chuckles as he stands up straight and puts his hands on my cheeks, stroking them with his thumbs. "In all fairness, you have been caged in this lonely house in the mountains. You have not had much opportunity to spend time in the company of males your own age. Perhaps I should not feel as special as that statement would imply."

I raise questioning brows to him. "Afraid you wouldn't stand up under competition?"

He chuckles again. "Perhaps. Suffice it to say, I am pleased not to face any."

"Not that I want to change the subject, but did you happen to check on Mom and Grandma?"

He nods and drops his hands back to his sides. "Yes, while you were brushing your teeth. They seem to have things well in hand. Your grandfather was quite surprised by the amount of Witch's bottles your mother has buried. He is having a tough time avoiding them."

Mom and her landmines. Apparently, she's been busy over the years. I wonder when she found the time to plant them when Zac and I wouldn't see her doing it. Come to think of it, she and Dad did spend a lot of time taking long walks in the woods. Maybe it was less walking and more burying.

"Is your circle still holding?"

"Yes. Your circle is still holding as well, even though it was hit by a car. If you were not connected physically to your protection spell, you would not have felt any of the things you have this morning. A side effect you should have been warned about. How are you feeling?"

I shrug. "I'm fine now. Nothing hurts, so I'm good."

"I was not speaking only of the physical sense."

I grimace. "Give me time to answer that one. Things are flying at me so fast; I can't keep up with my emotions."

Pulling me into his arms, he hugs me close, resting his chin on the top of my head. "I am afraid I understand that much too well. I felt the same way when I came here."

"You're doing that nice and sweet thing again."

"My apologies, I will try to work more derogatory statements and sarcasm into our conversations."

I can't help a small laugh. "Thank you, I appreciate it." Pushing away from him, I walk to my dresser. "I need to get out of these clothes. They have blood all over them."

"I will check on your father while you do that. I am afraid he will get caught in magical cross-fire."

I grimace. "Yeah, me too."

Kallen leaves and closes the door behind him. I pull out a pair of clean undies, jeans and a long sleeve dark blue tee from my drawers and change my clothes. Just as I pull the shirt over my head, I feel my skin start to tingle and I know the feeling of lightning striking is coming. I close my eyes and I'm no longer in my room. Have I mentioned how old this is getting? I'm back to not liking Grandma again, even if she didn't know this would happen. Oh well, at least I'm dressed. Ten seconds earlier and I would have been in the middle of this hotel room in just my bra.

Chapter 11

"Hallo, Xandra," the man in front of me drawls in what I think is supposed to be an English accent but he's not pulling it off well. He's just an inch or so taller than my five feet six inches and he's almost as big around as he is tall. His deep brown hair slicked back like only the bad guys on TV wear it, and his face is pock marked from what looks like many, many years of acne breakouts. Huh. As a Witch, you'd think he would have learned some sort of spell to prevent that from happening. Out of all the spells out there, one must exist to make someone less ugly. My belly button light is wrapped around his head, but it doesn't seem to hurt him as much as it did Beren. He doesn't even seem to be paying attention to it.

When I don't reply, he continues, "Your Grandfather is right, you do come when you're called. How lovely for us." Ah, that's why – he was expecting the rope light. I wonder if he's wearing some sort of amulet or something to block the pain.

I look down at the double bed next to me and there's a mirror tossed on the tacky flowered bedspread. I'm confused. "I thought Beren was the scryer."

The man in front of me laughs, and I get a magnificent view of how yellow his teeth are, and I can smell the garlic and onions he must have eaten recently on his breath. Gross, no grosser than gross. Ewww. Okay, I'm sure there must be some sort of magic which can help with *that*. Or maybe a toothbrush? No wonder Grandma thinks he needs to use magic to get women to like him.

"I may not have Beren's talent, but I am an efficient scryer. I'm certainly good enough to find a young Witch like you."

I wave my hand under my offended nostrils. "Do you think you could hold your hand over your mouth when you talk or something? I think I'm going to be sick if I have to keep smelling your breath." Rude yes, but oh so true. Between the blood I swallowed and his rancid breath, I really do feel nauseous.

"You impertinent little..." and then he seems to get control over his tongue and clamps his mouth closed for a heartbeat. When he opens it again, it's to say a spell. *"From my mind and from my heart, a feeling of wellbeing to you I impart. Led astray by family and foe, find safety here for your restless soul. I take from your heart your worries and pain; I cleanse your mind of its burden and strain. Heartbreak and sorrow await in the night, only in my presence will you find peace and light."*

It dawns on me as I listen to him drone on that I really should learn to interrupt Witches who are trying to work a spell against me instead of waiting to see if their spells have the desired effect. If only Mom and Dad hadn't taught me to be polite. Realizing the guy is now looking at me expectantly, my mouth forms into a broad smile.

"Excellent," he says. "You see, Louhi, I told you I would take her to task."

"Yes, I see."

The voice behind me startles me and I turn around quickly. Okay, interrupt Witches saying spells *and* look behind me. Crap, he could have knocked me out. Well, except for the fact that I'm not really here.

Louhi is older than the guy I figure must be Midar. He looks to be in his seventies, and where Midar is as big around as a three-hundred-year-old oak, Louhi is about as big around as a sapling. His yellow, papery skin stretches taut over his skeletal frame, and his eyes are sunken into dark caverns topped by a bushy uni-brow. His hair is a couple of wisps here and there, sticking out from his scalp in no particular pattern, and his nose looks like it's missing some cartilage. Ugly doesn't even begin to describe the man. He looks like he could have just walked off the screen of any number of horror flicks wielding an axe or a chainsaw. This is the guy who can put your mind in a happy place? I think he needs to put himself in a happy place, someplace far away from mirrors. Again, isn't there a spell for ugly??

"I don't believe you've been successful, Midar." Thin lips stretch over a row of perfectly straight white teeth that must be dentures. I think he's trying to smile and has failed miserably. He looks like his teeth ate his lips. The other man didn't scare me but this one does. I'm going to be seeing his creepy face in night-mares for years to come.

He might be a bit of a mind reader because he says as he gestures to himself, "This is what becomes of one who must carry the burdens of the minds of criminals, my dear. Not a pretty pic-ture, is it?"

"No." Yes, Mom and Dad taught me better manners than this, but they also taught me not to lie. Honesty won out this time.

A dry chuckle escapes his mouth. Or he was coughing. I'm not sure which. "Perhaps a fresh young mind like yours will reju-venate me. Shall we give it a try?"

I shake my head and unconsciously back up a step. "I'm sure I'd have the opposite effect. Mom always says I'm an old soul. I'd probably make you look worse." Oops, didn't mean to say that last part out loud.

His smile was iffy, but his snarl comes across perfectly clear as one side of his upper lip crawls up past his gums. "You do have a smart mouth, don't you? Perhaps I should stop wasting time and get on with it so we may all go home."

I don't know if I do it or if the protection spell does, but another rope of bright light shoots out towards Louhi and wraps around his head. The pressure it causes must be in direct proportion to how frightened I am because he grasps his head and falls to his knees as Beren did in the airport.

Midar hisses behind me. "You little minx, what are you doing to him?"

I turn towards Midar just as he's reaching out towards me. The light surges brighter and he's on his knees in a flash like Louhi. I need to get out of here. I'm getting way too freaked out by these guys. My eyelids slam together and in less than a heartbeat, I'm back in my own room kneeling in the middle of the floor. My breath is coming in harsh wheezes and there's sweat on my brow, but I'm safe and my mind is still intact.

"Xandra, are you alright?" Kallen asks through the door.

It takes me a second to catch my breath so I can answer him. "Yes," I finally manage.

Something in my voice must have clued him in. He opens the door, takes one look at me and rushes into the room. He immediately kneels in front of me and helps me lay down on the floor with my head on his lap so I can catch my breath and he can see my face. He wipes my damp forehead with the bottom of his shirt and asks, "What happened?"

"I met," my breathing is still too heavy to get more than one or two words out at a time. "Louhi." Breath. "And Midar." Am I having a panic attack?

Putting both his hands on my cheeks, he asks with real concern in his voice, "Are you alright? Did they harm you?"

I shake my head as my breathing begins to normalize. "No. But they scared the crap out of me. They're horrible looking!"

To my surprise, he leans back and his shoulders start moving with laughter. "They are horrible looking? You fight two Pooka warriors without flinching, but you are frightened by two old men because you do not like how they look?"

"You didn't see them," I pout knowing I sound ridiculous. "I'm going to have nightmares about them. Louhi especially."

This, of course, makes him laugh harder. "Then it is lucky for me that I did not see them. I would hate to have us both cowering in our sleep."

I glare at him, seriously considering pushing him over. I sit up so we are facing each other. "It's not funny."

"I disagree. I am quite amused."

That's it. I use the palms of my hands against his shoulders to push him backwards. What I didn't count on was him grabbing my arms and pulling me with him, so I end up sprawled on top of him. "Mm, much better," he says with a grin to my glowering face.

"I take it you've used up your nice and sweet allotment for the day?"

His eyes sparkle up at me. "I believe I may have even dipped into tomorrow's share."

"You're a jerk."

"You do like to point that out." I let out a small yelp when he rolls us over in a flash and I'm suddenly underneath him. He looks down at me with a smug grin. "Funny how you seem to like me anyway."

"Isn't it? I must have been dropped on my head when I was a baby."

With a good-natured laugh, he leans down and gives me a quick kiss before standing up and holding his hand out to me. I take it and let him pull me to my feet. "Now, I believe you should tell me a little bit more about these scary fellows you met."

I groan. I think there's more teasing coming my way. But they were horrible! "Grandpa told them I'm connected to the protection spell and if they scry for me, I come. Like a dog."

The teasing grin on his face has melted into concern again. "That is unfortunate. Have you tried simply not going to where the spell wants to take you?"

I roll my eyes. "No, because I'm a complete moron." All I get is an eyebrow raise in response to my sarcasm. "If I don't go, I feel like I'm being struck by lightning as long as they keep scrying for me."

"That does sound unpleasant."

"No, really, it's great. I'm actually starting to like it."

This time he narrows his eyes at me. "Being facetious is not helping."

No, but it makes me feel better. Unfortunately, he's right,

though. "What can we do?"

"We need to discover a method of counteracting that 'side effect.' Possibly channel it elsewhere."

That sounds painful for me. "How would we do that?"

A cunning smile creeps onto his lips. "Perhaps the rope of light you mentioned is for that purpose."

"Huh?"

"Perhaps you are meant to channel your pain through the rope of light. It is not meant to draw you out, but to punish whoever is attempting to call for you."

I frown at the thought. "So, I have to intentionally torture these people?" I don't mind giving them a little pain, but I'm not psychotic. Torturing people was not in my list of things I wanted to do when I grew up.

He gives me an assessing look. After a moment, he asks, "Did you think you would be able to get through this without intentionally hurting anyone?"

Yes, at least not torturing anyone. "No, I guess not."

"Are they not intentionally causing you harm?"

"I guess."

Those words barely leave my mouth when I'm zapped to my knees. Talk about perfect timing. If I must try to channel the pain through whoever is calling me, I hope it's Midar. I really didn't like him.

Kallen kneels in front of me as I'm trying to breathe through the pain. "Xandra, focus. Pull on your magic and use it to force the pain outward through the light. But you need to keep your mind here. Stay here with me."

Yeah, easy for him to say. He's not the one being French fried from the inside out. Regardless, I nod and focus on pulling magic from the earth. As it starts to fill me, the pain lessens, and I finally close my eyes.

I'm right back in the hotel room with the two scariest men I've ever met. They both have malicious little grins on their faces, and they look hungry. Are they planning to eat me for dinner? It wouldn't surprise me if their taste ran towards cannibalism. Maybe that's what made them so crazy in the first place.

Enough of that, I must focus. I look down at the light attached to me and then up at both of them. My magic takes over at this point. It recognizes a threat and immediately goes on the offense. The rope of light begins to glow brighter and hotter and within seconds, Midar and Louhi's simpering grins have contorted into twisted, pain filled sneers. But I feel great. Not an ounce of pain left in me.

Both men are on their knees holding their heads. Louhi looks up and growls, "You will not hold us like this for long. We have defenses against your kind of magic."

My brows crawl up to my hairline. "Then why would you call me – twice – without using them?" I shake my head. "To think, you're part of Grandpa's brain trust. I let you off the first time without any real pain, and this time I'm going to let you off with a warning. If you call for me again, I will not be so nice. Leave me and my family alone. I really don't want to hurt you and I'm not going to hurt anyone else with my power. The 'so called' prophecy will not happen. Leave. Me. Alone."

With a final push of my magic through the light, I pull it back. Midar has a shadow in his eyes that looks an awful lot like fear. Louhi simply looks more determined and angrier. Guess I'll have to wait and see how that plays out but I'm not staying here a second longer. I close my eyes and don't open them until I hear Kallen's voice and feel his hands on my shoulders. A look of relief washes over his face.

"Xandra, are you alright?"

Opening my eyes slowly, I smile. "Yes."

"Was it the same two men?"

I nod. "Yeah, Louhi and Midar, and yes, they're still just as horrible looking."

That causes him to chuckle. "I assume you were successful in channeling the pain?"

"Yup, and they didn't like it at all. Midar was scared, but I think I just made Louhi really mad. He said they have protection against 'my kind of magic,' whatever that means."

"I am sure he meant Fairy magic."

Oh, that makes sense. "Could they really have things that would make them immune to Fairy magic?"

He shakes his head. "No. They may have talismans or amulets which will temporarily repel Fairy magic, but nothing that would protect them indefinitely."

That's good. I'd hate to have to rely on only my Witch magic. Who knows what collateral damage it could cause?

Kallen gets to his feet and holds his hand out to me. "Come."

"You know I hate it when you treat me like a dog."

He looks confused and I roll my eyes. "When you tell me to 'come' it sounds like a command for a dog. I'm not a dog. Calling me like one is what those guys are doing, I don't what my boy-friend doing it, too."

Now he's angry. Maybe I went a little far comparing him to Midar and Louhi, but I'm on edge myself. "Am I supposed to beg you on humbled knee? Perhaps I should prostrate myself in front of you? Would that be better?" Before I can say the cutting retort that is parked on my tongue, he snaps, "We should find the others and tell them what you have succeeded in doing." He walks out the door and down the hall.

Geez, he sure is sensitive. Or I seriously owe him an apology. Yeah, probably that. With heavy feet, I follow him out into the hall towards the kitchen.

Mom and Grandma are back inside. Mom's face is grim. "Xandra, there you are. I was just discussing with your father and grand-mother *how* changed your grandfather is. It's as if he's not even the same man he was when I was growing up." She shakes her head. "I don't know *who* this man is. He's become a monster." She turns to Grandma. "You tried to tell me, but I didn't believe you."

"He has slowly morphed into this shell of a man. It's been a long time since I could stand to be in his presence."

"Is he under a spell?" I ask.

Grandma looks startled. "Sveargith is too strong to be influenced in such a way."

I shrug. "Unless his defenses were down. Maybe losing both you and Mom was enough for someone to sneak in and put him under a spell. It could happen, couldn't it?" I don't know that I believe it, but maybe it'll make them feel better to think that's the case.

Mom's big blue eyes are full of hope. "Yes, if he was depressed enough, it may have given someone an in. Don't you think, Mother?"

Grandma still looks doubtful. "Why would someone do that?"

"Power, love, money. Aren't those the usual things people are after when they do things like that?"

Dad pipes up from where he's floating next to Mom. "But why not just take over. Why keep him in place at all?"

"Perhaps whoever is exerting control over him is not powerful enough to hold the throne on his or her own," Kallen says.

"And needs my father's strength in order to rule over the realm."

"So, Grandpa's like a puppet, then?"

Kallen nods. "It is a distinct possibility if the changes in him have been as dramatic as your mother and grandmother claim."

"Is it just as likely that he's become a bitter old man because both his daughter and his wife left him?" Okay, I know I started this conversation and was trying to be optimistic, but we should look at all the options.

Kallen is giving me a weird look for my backpedaling but Grandma speaks up before he has a chance. "It could be. But being under a spell would better account for his radical behavior changes over the years. I guess I have been too close to the situation. I've wondered if the Witan had too much power over the years, but it didn't dawn on me they might actually be controlling Sveargith."

"They could do that?" I ask in a small voice.

Kallen nods. "Yes, even the most powerful Witch can be spelled if his or her psychic defenses are low enough."

That's what I'm afraid of. I don't want Grandpa to be under a spell because that means I just might be vulnerable as well. As soon as someone in my family is threatened, or Kallen, my mental defenses will come tumbling down. Kallen's pretty smart. He seems to catch on to my fear and despite his annoyance from a few minutes ago, he comes to stand by my side and slips my hand in his.

He gives my hand a little squeeze. "If your grandfather is under a spell, it was probably years in the making. The influence would have been so subtle, he would not have even been aware of the change."

That is not comforting at all. "Which means he's not struggling against it. He just accepts it as the person he's become? He doesn't realize there's anything wrong with him."

"From what your grandmother says, these Witches are exceptionally good at planting emotions and controlling others. It is not unreasonable to assume they can be subtle when the situation requires it."

"Indeed." Grandma looks contemplative. Can this idea really have just dawned on her? Seriously, she's been near him all these years. As if reading my thoughts, she says, "I should have paid better attention to the changes Sveargith underwent. I was so focused on his part in chasing my daughter away, I lost sight of everything else around me."

"Where is Grandpa now?"

"He left. But I'm sure he'll be back soon."

Yeah, I'm sure he will be.

Chapter 12

I think if I put one more necklace around my neck with an amulet or talisman on it, I'm not going to be able to stand up from my chair. I must be wearing at least fifty pounds of the things made of rocks, silver, amber, leather and who knows what else. Mom and Grandma have been going crazy for the last three hours making them in preparation for the attack of Grandpa and the Witan. I still can't keep track of what all these things do; I'm just taking their word for it that I need them. There's one that smells particularly foul, though. Kallen's been keeping his distance since I put that one on. I'm tempted to slip off to the bathroom and accidently flush it down the toilet. Mom's pretty focused on other things right now, maybe she wouldn't notice.

Dad and Kallen are still taking turns patrolling the outside of the house. Dad has strict orders from Mom not to leave the area of the protection circles, though. She's afraid Fatin will actually try to exorcise him.

Louhi and Midar must have warned the others not to scry for me because I haven't felt their pull since the last encounter when I figured out that my glowing rope can be used as a weapon of pain. None of us find it particularly comforting, though. It probably just means they're thinking of worse things to do to me. My overactive imagination has been running through possible scenarios, and none of them turn out well for me. I'm not as certain as I was yesterday morning that I can stand up to these people and win. They fight too dirty. Thank goodness I don't have to do it alone.

I'm in the middle of a daydream where Grandpa creates a fire-bomb out of thin air so when Kallen's hand touches my shoulder, I practically jump off my chair. Without even consciously thinking about it, I'm flooded with magic, which makes everyone in the room stop what they're doing except Dad. He's oblivious. Kallen takes several steps back and holds his hands up in front of him in an 'I come in peace' gesture. Color rushes to my cheeks as I try to keep the magic under control. Several deep breaths later, I've let it all go.

Mom reaches across the table and touches my hand with her cold one. "You'll be fine. Your grandmother and Kallen and I won't let anything happen to you." Mom's always been perceptive when it came to me and Zac. But then again, even the least perceptive person in the world could figure out that I'm worried about dying in the next day or two.

The sudden ringing of the phone almost causes the same reaction as Kallen's touch. Magic starts flooding into me again. At this rate, the biggest danger to all of us is going to be me.

Looks are exchanged around the room as we all hesitate, not wanting to answer the call. After the sixth ring, I can't take it anymore and I answer it. We might as well get this over with. "Hello."

"Xandra, is your mom or dad around?" It's Aunt Barb.

"We're here, Barb. What's going on?" Dad asks from his position next to Mom where he's been watching in fascination as Mom works her spells.

"I just got the strangest phone call. A Dr. Louis just called. He said he was an old friend of yours from medical school and he was hoping to drop by while he was in Denver."

Any color Mom or Dad had has left them. I take it Dad didn't go to school with a Dr. Louis. Or a Dr. Louhi, maybe. "Barb," Mom says with a voice that's shakier than I care to hear, "you and Zac need to get out of there as soon as possible. Get in your car and drive. Right now." It's my turn to lose all my color. They've found Aunt Barb and Zac.

"Julienne, what's wrong? What's going on?"

"How did they know?" I ask Mom, who at the moment looks like someone poked a hole in her sanity balloon and all the air is leaking out. I don't know if she's going to be able to hold it together much longer. Maybe now's not the best time to ask her questions. "Um, Aunt Barb, you should do what Mom's asking. We can explain later. Just go."

"Okay," she says and the tremor in her voice tells me she's finally getting how serious this is. "Should I pack anything?"

"NO! Just go!" Mom yells. Nope, not much air left in that sanity balloon.

Aunt Barb gasps in shock but she doesn't ask any more questions. "Alright, we're on our way out now. Zac, get your shoes and your coat, we have to go."

We can hear Zac in the background asking his own questions, but Aunt Barb shushes him. I can imagine the pouty look on his face after being scolded for asking reasonable questions. I feel horrible he must go through all of this because of me. No, because of Grandpa.

"Zac. Shoes. Now." Aunt Barb tells him and then we hear her sharp intake of breath. "Jim, there's someone at the door. What do I do?"

Five voices answer her at once. "Don't answer it!"

Panic in his voice, Dad asks, "Barb, can you go out the fire escape?"

"I don't know. Zac," she whispers, "we need to try to go out the fire escape."

"Cool!" we hear Zac say and a smile tries to touch my lips but I'm too worried about them for it to get very far.

"Okay, I'm trying to get the window open now. It's stuck. Zac, come here and help me." We hear them struggling to get the window open and a little pop tells us when they're successful.

"Barb, look below, is there anyone there?" Dad instructs.

After a second, she gasps. "There's a rather large man staring up here."

"They are trapped," Kallen says grimly.

It's the Fairies all over again. They're going to use my brother, and my aunt this time, to try to get me to surrender to them. I'm an hour and a half away so I can't do anything about it.

Aunt Barb begins whispering frantically into the phone. "Oh god, Jim, someone just opened the door. Zac, get in the closet. Hurry!"

The closet? That's the first place they'll look. My eyes close in defeat because I know it'll be any minute now that they're captured. For several long heartbeats, all we can hear is Aunt Barb's jagged breaths as she tries to swallow her fear.

Every second that passes increases the amount of magic that is saturating my body. My ears strain to hear the telltale sounds that will let us know that Zac and Aunt Barb have been found, and my body prepares for a fight too far away to win. Every nerve ending I have is tingling and suddenly my mind is aglow with a burning white light that sears through me. My eyes open like shutters and my voice forces my mouth to open for the scream that pierces the air. I can't see the kitchen, I can't see the four people in the room with me, all I can see is white and it's blinding me, but my eyes refuse to close.

I'm pulled forward, a tugging that starts around my middle, as the light fades and my eyes start to focus. I'm not in my kitchen any longer. I'm in Denver, and directly in front of me is the source of my wrath. Maeva. Grandpa. Louhi. Their expressions tell me they weren't expecting me.

Maeva gasps. "We didn't tell you to come."

Like snakes uncoiling, three ropes of light lash out and find their targets. My voice comes out in an angry snarl. "I am not a dog; I can come and go as I please." Pain races across their faces, contorting Louhi's into something resembling a caricature of a monster right out of a B horror movie.

Grandpa is fumbling with something around his neck as he fights the pain. "Invoke the spell!" he shouts to get the attention of the other two. Maeva is on the ground now but Louhi is still struggling to stand like Grandpa. Another surge of energy rushes through me and they are both forced to their knees.

Finally, Grandpa has freed a necklace from his collar that looks to be made of silver, amber and iron. A Fairy repellant. I know that one because Mom gave me one to protect me from the Fairies. Oh, he's going to be mad when he figures out those don't work on me. *"Fire and air surround, earth and water abound. I in She and She in me, true goddess of the earth and sea, protect us from this Fae so foul, shield us from her reckless power."*

Okay, first of all, that last part didn't rhyme. And second, did he just call me foul? Now I'm really mad. I focus my thoughts on the talisman he holds in his hand and Grandpa falls backwards as it explodes, trying to shield himself from the flames. "I am so tired of you thinking you're better than me! If anyone is foul, it's you three. All I'm trying to do is live my life, but you guys come after me like I've set a house of kittens on fire or something! Alright, if you want a fight, you've got it. But you will leave my Aunt and my brother alone. If you harm one spec on their body, I won't even bother trying to hold back my magic because this," I gesture at the lights keeping them glued to their spots, "is nothing compared to what I can do if I get really mad. Now sleep." Instantly, three bodies tumble to the ground in a heap, sound asleep.

"Aunt Barb, Zac, you can come out now!" I call. I'm not sure which room they're in.

"Xandra!" I hear Zac call and suddenly he's bounding down the hall towards me. He stops short when his mind finally registers what he's seeing. "You're glowing." There's more admiration in his voice than fear. "Why are you glowing? Are you a ghost now, too?" How much does it say about our lives that he would be so calm and accepting about that?

"No, but I'm not really here, either. Just my mind is."

His eyes light up with excitement. "Can I do that?"

I can't help but be amused. "No, sorry."

Aunt Barb has joined him in the hallway. "Xandra, you're astral projecting! I knew it could be done." She has been working on that theory since Mom and Dad became ghosts and she had positive proof that spirits can survive outside the body. "I wish I had my equipment here."

Even with all the craziness going on, she's still a scientist at heart. "You two need to hurry. Get in your car and drive home as fast as the roads will let you."

"What about them?" She gestures to the sleeping bodies on the floor.

"They'll be out for as long as I'm here, and if the other one is at the back of the building, he shouldn't see you leave. But I don't know how long he'll wait before he comes looking for his friends, so go, now."

She nods and hurries to the front closet to get their coats. She throws Zac his dark blue and gray Columbia ski jacket and she slips into her heavy beige trench coat. When they finally have their boots, hats, and gloves on, I shoo them out the door. I'm not going anywhere until I at least know they're on the road to safety. It's going to be a long hour and a half waiting for them to arrive back at the house.

As I watch them get into the car from the front apartment window, I begin to feel my rage lessen. My skin isn't tingling anymore, and the ropes of light have recoiled. It's time to go back home.

Chapter 13

D id I mention how disconcerting it is to pass out one place and wake up another? I think I'm on the couch this time and I'm seriously debating whether I want to open my eyes. I don't want to know what I did to the house this time. Plus, keeping my eyes closed allows me to eavesdrop on the hushed conversation Kallen and Grandma seem to be having.

"This shouldn't be happening."

"Whether it should be or not, it is. How do we stop it?"

"I don't know. In all my years, this has never happened. I knew when I fell that my magic wouldn't be as strong. It should be a protection circle, nothing more."

"But she has not fallen. Therein may lay the problem."

"No, it shouldn't make a difference. Her blood should be weakened regardless."

"Has there ever been such a magical mixing of blood?"

I crack my eyes open just a tiny bit because Grandma doesn't answer him right away. The two of them are in the corner of the room with their heads together. Which looks odd because Kallen is a foot taller than she is, so his shoulders are stooped way over. I wonder what the chances are they'll keep talking when they find out I'm awake?

Unfortunately, I find out right away because Kallen turns his head before I have a chance to close my eyes. I never was very sneaky. It only takes him two strides to get to the couch and he kneels next to me. "Do you think you could manage to go a little longer between attempts to drive us out of our minds with worry?" He smiles but the lines on his forehead tell me just how concerned he has been.

"Sorry, I have to meet my quota. If I don't do it at least three times a day, they'll revoke my magic license."

His eyebrows rise skeptically. "And who, exactly, would give *you* a license to practice magic?"

"I have connections in high places. I am related to kings, you know."

His smile is a little brighter now and he inclines his head. "Yet you deign to be in the company of a lowly peasant such as myself. How fortunate I am."

"I hate to interrupt," Grandma says softly over Kallen's shoulder, "but how are you feeling, dear?"

"Other than a bit of a headache, I feel fine. How long have I been out?"

Kallen pushes a strand of hair behind my ear. "Only an hour this time. Just long enough for me to reverse your wild magic."

I groan. "What did I do this time?"

Grandma gives him a dirty look. "Nothing that couldn't be fixed." Turning back to me, she says, "The important thing is figuring out what happened to you."

I sit up slowly and put a hand to my aching head. "I went to Denver."

A vein on the side of Kallen's head starts to throb as his face contorts in anger. "Did they scry for you again with a stronger spell?"

I shake my head but that makes it hurt more so I immediately stop. "No, apparently, I can go without them scrying for me."

He shoots Grandma a questioning look and she shrugs her shoulders. Apparently, she didn't know I could do that, either. Maybe Grandma should have investigated this whole protection spell thing a little bit more before having me start marking trees with my blood. "So, any chance you two want to tell me what you were whispering about?"

Kallen's face immediately becomes blank. Grandma tries for the same look but it's those worry lines around her eyes that give her a way. My own face sets like stone. "Uh huh, that's what I thought." I push off the couch to make a dramatic exit. Of course, I fall right back against the cushions which makes my head hurt even more. If Kallen let's that smirk he's fighting against surface, I swear I'm going to kick him in the shins.

"Perhaps you should lie down for a few more minutes," Grandma says. She looks relieved to have something come up to change the subject.

"Fine." But I'm not happy about it. "Where are Mom and Dad?"

"Your mother is looking for any sign of your Grandfather or the Witan. We figured they must be close if they scried for you again."

"No, they were all in Denver going after Zac and Aunt Barb. How do you think they found them?"

Grandma's lips slam together in a grim line for a moment before she answers. "They do not rely entirely on their magic to find people. They also use high tech gadgets such as phone bugs. Your grandfather planted one while he was here."

My face can't even begin to contort in a way that would show exactly how shocked and angry I am. "You waited until *now* to bring this up? Don't you think we should have known they did things like this *before* we let them listen in on our phone calls? You put Aunt Barb and Zac in danger!" I didn't even realize I had stood up and stalked Grandma across the room until her back hit the wall. I flinch when Kallen puts his hands on my shoulders to keep me from getting closer to her.

"Xandra, your father has already been through this with your grandmother," he says gently, pulling me back into him and putting his arms around my waist. I'm not sure if it's a sign of affection or restraint. Probably both considering how volatile I've been the last two days.

"I am so sorry. It never even dawned on me they would use anything other than magic. I'm afraid I've kept myself too ignorant of the methods they use to track errant Witches."

I can't help asking, "What, exactly, *have* you paid attention to over the last eighteen years?"

She looks like her spirit has left her as her shoulders sag and the weight of all her years show on her face like a treasure map of tragedy. "Hardly anything," she says just above a whisper.

Well, how can I stay mad at her now that she looks so pathetic? I growl in frustration and walk out of Kallen's arms. I keep walking until I reach the bathroom and I go in and slam the door. I turn the water in the sink on and lean my hands on the counter and my forehead against the cool of the mirror. Several deep breaths later and I can start pushing the magic that rushed into me back into the earth.

It doesn't take long for there to be a knock on the door. "Go away," I growl. I don't know if it is Kallen or Grandma, and at the moment, I don't care. I need a couple of minutes alone. Whoever it is doesn't knock again.

I'm not even sure why I'm crying. I thought I had come to terms with this whole mess. Apparently not.

An icy cold hand touches my back. "Honey, are you alright?"

I push back so I'm standing up straight and wipe my eyes before meeting Mom's in the mirror. I'm always amazed that she has a reflection, since most light goes right through her instead of being reflected. "Yeah, I'm okay. I just kinda lost it for a minute."

"Considering what you've been through recently, I've been impressed by how well you've stood up under the pressure. But I'm also concerned that you feel like you need to be so stoical all the time. It's okay to let your feelings out like this. You don't have to keep them all bottled up, and you don't have to lock yourself in the bathroom to breakdown. We are all here for you."

"I know." I wipe the last of the tears away and try to smile.

Mom lays her chilly hand on my cheek and it feels good. "Do you think you could tell us what happened? Are Aunt Barb and Zac okay?"

That's right, I haven't told them anything yet. "Yes, they're fine. They're on their way here. But Mom, can I have just a few minutes before I sit down with everyone?"

"Certainly. Now that I know your brother is okay, I can wait a few minutes for the details. You have Kallen awfully worried, though. I think he's going to wear holes in the floor if he keeps pacing as he has been. But I am impressed by how much he seems to care about you."

A real smile touches my lips. "I told you he's a nice guy."

Mom chuckles. "Let's just say he has his moments and leave it at that. I'm going to let your father know Zac and his sister are fine. You come out when you're ready." She floats back through the door leaving me to collect myself.

I splash some cold water on my face and brush my teeth again. Everything feels better if you have clean teeth, right? With a last deep breath and look in the mirror to make sure my eyes aren't too puffy, I open the door to face the rest of the day.

Chapter 14

Mom's right, Kallen is going to pace a hole through the floor. It takes him a moment before he realizes I'm in the room and when he does, he comes to a halt. "How are you?" he asks.

Somehow, I'm able to muster a real smile and he visibly relaxes. "Ready for the next fight."

"How about you fill in the details of the last one before starting on the next," Dad says from the counter near the stove. Grandma made coffee and he's soaking in the scent. Dad really misses food.

"Okay." Grabbing a banana off the counter first, I sit down at the table and fill them in on my trip to Denver.

Dad's the first one to speak. "So, you can project your consciousness wherever you want?"

I shrug. "I don't know. I haven't tried to go anywhere else unless the Witan scried for me."

He looks at Grandma. "Did you know she'd be able to do this?"

She shakes her head. "I have no idea why she is capable of any of this. It's not how it's supposed to work."

Dad sets his mouth in a grim line. I suspect he's already told her what he thinks about her lack of knowledge. Probably several times.

Wanting to steer the conversation back to something less volatile, I ask, "What did I do to the kitchen?" Okay, Dad's glaring even harder at Grandma now. Maybe this isn't a less volatile subject.

The room is suddenly quiet. Too quiet. Kallen looks at the other three people in the room to see if they're going to make him tell me. Yup, they sure are. With a resigned look, he turns back to me. "You blinded us."

No way. "What are you talking about? You can all see, can't you?"

"Yes, we can *now*," he says as if I'm a toddler. "An hour ago, it was a different story."

I still don't believe him. "How on earth could I have blinded all of you?"

Now that the hard part is out of the way, Grandma joins the conversation. "It was as if your magic became pure light and we were not prepared to shield against it."

"It caused flash blindness," Dad explains. "It burned our retinas. My guess would be, considering the effect on your grandmother and Kallen, the intensity was around that of a nuclear explosion. It even affected your mother and me."

"If Kallen hadn't immediately harnessed his magic to create another protection circle here in the kitchen, the effect could have been permanent," Mom says quietly. I think she's afraid she's going to upset me again.

She doesn't. I can't change what happened so there's nothing to do but move forward. "See, another good reason he stayed here," I say with a smile in his direction.

Mom chuckles now that she knows the news isn't going to permanently damage my psyche. "Yes, I suppose it is."

Kallen's quiet, but he has a smile of his own. At least, he does until he tells me the next part of the bad news. "Yes, the blindness was temporary but there's more. Before your aunt and brother arrive, we have to let down our protection circles."

"What?" I am positive I didn't hear him correctly.

"Before your aunt and brother arrive, we have to let down our protection circles," he says as if I didn't hear him the first time.

I roll my eyes. "I heard you. Why?"

"Because your circle creates a physical barrier, they will not be able to cross, and my protection circle makes the area within sit between realms which cannot be seen from either. To them, it would appear as if the house is not here and they would not be able to locate it."

Stupid protection circles. They're becoming a lot more of a hassle than they're supposed to be. I can handle this. I just need to breathe. A lot. Well, not this much. I might hyperventilate. "Okay," I say slowly. "What do we do if the Witan attack while the circles are down?"

"Hopefully, we will be able to hold them off."

"Hopefully. That's comforting," I mumble.

"I've called Barb and they're only about fifteen minutes away," Dad says. "Whatever we're going to do, we need to hurry."

"You do realize Grandpa and the Witan could be right behind them, right? My magic that was keeping them asleep retracted when I left Aunt Barb's apartment."

Grandma nods glumly. "Yes, we're assuming they are."

Great. Fantastic. This isn't going to be ugly at all. But I'm not going to let it get me down. I'm going to move forward. "What do I have to do to lower the protection circle?" I ask Grandma.

"It's quite simple. You need to mix your blood with the clay again and draw a line through the pentacle."

Wonderful, more of my blood going into a spell. Maybe I should create my own blood bank. "Let's do it then. I don't want Aunt Barb driving into it."

I get up from the table and walk to the door where I left my boots earlier. I slip them on, but I don't bother with a coat. If all I need to do is draw a line, I'm not going to be out there long. Pulling the door open, I go outside. I assume Grandma's following with her slimy clay.

When I'm next to the elder, I take Mom's athame from Grandma and poke my finger. I let the blood drip into the clay and then I use my finger to stir it a little. This stuff is so nasty. I know I'm never going to get it all out from under my fingernails.

With a glob of clay on my finger, I draw a line through the pentacle. Once I do, a rush of magic hits me so hard and fast that I'm flung about twenty feet back towards the house. Thank god there weren't any trees in the way. I've already had a broken rib from slamming into a tree because of magic.

As I lie in the snow wishing I had worn my coat, the magic seems to hover over me instead of rushing back to the earth. I try willing it back, but it won't go. That's not a good sign.

Kallen must be thinking the same thing. "Xandra, are you going to let it go?" he asks from the elder tree. I don't blame him for not wanting to get closer with this much magic hanging around. Literally.

"I'm trying," I say. The snow under me is making my clothes uncomfortably wet, making me even colder, but I don't think I can get up. I try to move to a sitting position but nope, can't budge. "Um, anyone have any suggestions about how I can get this magic off me?"

"Magic is not an elephant. It cannot sit on you and hold you down."

I glare up at him. "Well, apparently mine is because it won't budge."

Mom puts her hand over her face to hide her smile. "It's not funny," I tell her including her in my glare as well.

"Have you tried simply returning the magic to the earth?" Kallen asks in that lovely condescending voice of his.

"Was I just saying it's good that you stayed? I'm seriously reconsidering that opinion at the moment."

"Be that as it may, you are the only one who can return this magic to the earth."

"Really? Because I thought little elves came along and did it for me." Me, sarcastic? Nah. Another thought hits me. "Isn't this the same magic that knocked me out cold for almost a day? What if I take it all back through me and it does the same thing again?"

Huh, I seem to have stumped him on that one. Not even the tiniest bit of condescension on his face now. Mom's not laughing anymore, either.

Grandma's the first to respond. She looks thoughtful as she says,

"It very well could be that your mind and body are refusing to process the magic for that reason."

"Mother, I've never heard of such a thing," Mom admonishes gently. I don't know, it seems plausible to me.

Grandma shrugs and shakes her head. "Your daughter is an enigma, Julienne. Who is to say it doesn't work that way for *her*?" Now Mom looks stumped, too.

"Hey, can we have the philosophical debate later and right now figure out what I'm supposed to do? I think my back is getting frostbitten."

"You are literally pinned down by your own magic?" Kallen asks as if he still doesn't believe it. Well, that's annoying.

"Yes, I am literally pinned down. As in, I can't get up. As in, there is a large amount of magic hovering over me like a giant elephant butt about to sit on me. Would you like me to paint a better picture of it or is it pretty clear now that I'm being pinned down by my magic?"

He narrows his eyes at me and says dryly, "Yes, the mental image is perfectly clear now, thank you."

I'm about to say something else, maybe apologize for being so snippy, when there's the unmistakable sound of tires on gravel and snow. Please let that be Aunt Barb and not the Witan. Is it possible to get that lucky while I'm being held captive by my magic? That's a no brainer. Of course not. The car slows as it approaches the driveway and then stops.

"Oh my god," Mom whispers. "It's Fatin."

They can see the driveway from where they're standing but I can't from where I'm lying. I need to get up. Now if I can only get this magic to understand that. I roll over onto my side, just barely and with much effort, and then flop onto my belly. But I still can't get up. All I managed to do is get the other side of my clothes snowy and cold.

"Quillian, Athear, you know what needs to be done," a smooth, deep voice says. "Please don't make this harder than it needs to be."

Why do the bad guys always say that? Do they really think people are just going to roll over and let them do exactly what they want to do? Okay, well, I guess that's a bad analogy, because in this case, the only thing I can do right now is roll over, but that's not the point.

"Stay here," Grandma says quietly to Mom and Dad. Mom looks like she's about to refuse until she glances over at Dad. Then she nods. Her face fills with fear – I'm assuming at the thought of him being exorcised. Ultimately, she lets Grandma and Kallen walk towards Fatin without her.

"This is the Fairy I've heard so much about? He is a tall one, isn't he?" There's not a hint of distress in Fatin's voice. "Athear, you know how this is going to play out. I'm going to threaten your daughter and her husband, and then you and the Fairy are going to try to stop me, and things are going to get tedious from there. I was hoping to avoid all of this, which is why I haven't made my presence known until now. But, alas, here I am, and we both know, Athear, the Witan never loses. Are you willing to lose both the daughter you have mourned for the last eighteen years as well as the sin against nature we seek?"

"The only sins against nature are you lot who have abused your power over the years. Xandra has committed no crime. You have no business here and as queen, I demand that you leave." Grandma's voice is even, but there is definitely an underlying threat in it.

Which Fatin ignores. "You haven't really served as our queen for these past eighteen years, now have you, Athear. Nor are you a member of the Witan, so you don't get a vote. You may offer your opinion, which you have done on several occasions, and it was taken into consideration. Then we voted to disregard it."

"The Witan seem to disregard any opinions other than their own, Fatin. You're not exactly what could be called a fair and impartial jury, now are you," Grandma says in the same patronizing tone Fatin had used.

"We keep the world safe from those who would cause harm, Athear. Nothing more than that."

The distinctive sound of tires on gravel and snow can be heard again, cutting off whatever Grandma is about to say. Okay, this is crazy; I really need to stand up. I push my hands against the snow-covered ground but it's no good. I'm still trapped.

"Ah, finally," Fatin says. "I knew they couldn't be too far behind."

He can only mean Aunt Barb and Zac. He specializes in ghosts; he can't hurt them. Right? I can dream, can't I?

Grandma's gasp is my first clue that things aren't right. "Surprised, Athear? It was a simple matter for Beren and Davina to find them and compel them to give themselves up."

The Witan have Aunt Barb and Zac. I didn't even think about the fact that they could be tracked. I should have stayed in Denver until they had enough time to safely reach us. This is all my fault.

"Have you hurt them?" Kallen asks. His voice is completely void of emotion, not like mine would be if I were over there. I must get up. I push harder and I can get to my hands and knees, but the magic is pushing hard against my back.

"We have no wish to harm them," Fatin says. "We simply want to offer a trade."

Kallen's voice turns to steel. "Trade one death for another, how sporting of you."

There's the sound of car doors closing, and I can hear muffled screams coming from Aunt Barb and Zac. They must have them gagged. Mom and Dad rush past me, no longer willing to hide behind Grandma and Kallen. It's my job to protect them and here I am struggling with my own magic, defeating myself.

"Ah, Quillian, how lovely to see you again," Fatin purrs. Eew, it kind of sounds like he has a thing for Mom. So many reasons it's good she left home.

"Let our son and my sister go," Dad demands in his best 'I'm going to kill you the first chance I get' voice.

"We would like nothing better." I know that gravelly, my teeth are going to fall out of my mouth soon, voice. It's Louhi. Great, the whole gang is here. I push harder and I'm able to kneel.

"Sveargith, you know this is wrong. You're the king, you can make this stop," Grandma pleads. That must have cost her a lot of pride considering how much she dislikes Grandpa now.

"The Witan has made a ruling. King Sveargith is unable to change it on his own," Maeva says in a catty voice. "Your pleas will do no good, Athear." She says Grandma's name like she rolled it around on her tongue and found out it had dirt on it.

"Athear, you have to understand," Grandpa says, and he sounds unsure, like he's wavering.

"I do not have to understand. You are being led around like a stray dog by these Witches." Hmm, she says Witches the same way Maeva had said her name. I have one leg with my foot on the ground and I'm getting closer to being able to stand up.

"Enough of this talk," Midar growls. Actually, it sounds more like a whine, but I think he was trying to sound like he growled. He's just not a tough sounding man, especially with the fake English accent he tries to pull off. I'm on my feet now but walking seems like a task far beyond my capabilities. "Where is the girl?"

"You will have to go through me to get her." Okay, Kallen is rather good at growling.

"I'm not afraid of you, Fairy." I don't know, he sounds pretty scared.

"Davina, get your hands off my son." Mom's surprisingly good with the growl, too. Poor Midar, he's way out of his depth right now.

"Spirit in unrest, soul in pain, come to me, find peace again. Leave this world of longing and woe, sorrow filled days no longer you'll know..."

"Jim, no," Mom cries followed by a scream from one of the women in the driveway.

"Focus on the Fairy!" Fatin shouts. He sounds muffled and farther away. Is he hiding behind a tree at the end of the driveway or something? I put a foot forward and I'm able to take a step. My legs are shaky, and I feel as if I have the weight of the world on my back, but I'm moving forward.

An explosion rocks the ground. Actually, it's several explosions. Must be more of Mom's Witch Bottles. Seriously, when did she have time to do all that? The earth shaking just that little bit is enough to bring me to my knees again. Why won't this magic let me go? I swear, I am never trying one of Grandma's spells again.

"Kallen, watch out!" Grandma yells.

"Child, hold still!" I think that was Beren. Good for Zac, he's fighting against him.

"He has some sort of dart!"

"Get behind the cars!"

Kallen has Fairy darts. They can bring down a Fairy so they can certainly bring down a Witch. They don't work on me, though. They just make me feel drunk. This is so frustrating. I need to get over there and join the fight. They need me. I'm on my feet again but walking isn't getting any easier.

"Let Jim and Zac go!" Mom yells. "Or I swear, I will blow this entire area away. Kallen, they're setting a trap for you, make a circle." Oh god, Fatin has control over Dad, Beren has Zac and now they're going after Kallen. I've taken four steps now. I can do this.

"Mom, help!" Zac sounds so scared.

"Shut up," Beren snarls and I hear a sickening smack. I'm fairly certain he just hit Zac. Are you kidding me? Who hits a little boy?

"What have you done? Zac, wake up!" Mom cries.

"The Fairy's down, finish him off!"

They are hurting Dad, Zac and now Kallen! No way! Not happening! With the force of a hurricane, the magic comes into me. The pain is immense for several seconds, like someone has stabbed me in the back – twice. The magic rushes through me and I feel how a bolt of lightning must feel. I'm awash with electricity. The air is crackling around me, and I am now able to walk freely towards the melee in the driveway.

As soon as I round the house, it's not just electricity I'm awash with. Anger surges through me and suddenly I'm seeing the action in slow motion. Kallen is on his knees and looks to be in a great deal of pain as a complicated web of magic immobilizes him. Aunt Barb is sitting in the snow with her arms and legs bound and a gag still in her mouth. Dad is hovering near Fatin and has an eerily blank face. Grandma is defending herself from a spell that is coming from either Maeva or Davina. My money's on Maeva. Then there's Zac. My precious little brother with his sandy brown hair and blue eyes like Mom and Dad is lying in the snow. Tossed aside like he no longer matters. His eyes are closed, and I don't know if he's alive or not. His skin is so pale, and his small chest is still.

All at once, time catches up and my senses are flooded. It's too much; I need to expend some of this energy. Focusing on a tree behind the two black cars in the driveway, it explodes in a shower of wood the size of toothpicks. That gets everyone's attention. Now, all eyes are on me. Wide, shocked eyes. Did they think I wouldn't join the fight?

As I walk past Kallen, I run my hand through the web of magic. It dissolves like cotton candy in the rain. He falls to his hands and knees and takes gasping breaths as his body recovers from the stress and pain. I keep walking.

Finally, I'm in front of Zac. I kneel in the snow and gather him in my arms and press my cheek to his chest. He's breathing, but barely.

I look up and my eyes meet Louhi's. I can see the cruelty that lives in his soul. The curl of his lips tells me he's been waiting for this moment for eighteen years. I'm on my knees in front of him and he thinks he holds all the cards. Silly man, I just came for my brother.

"Say the spell," he says, his voice filled with the glee of someone who believes he has won. "Kill them all."

Seven voices begin to chant. *"From ancient times of rhymes and runes, these witches call upon the power of the moon to scourge the earth of magic black, and within its womb to take mercifully back, this one born in heresy and shame, and those who've shielded her also to blame, swallow their guilt and show us their pain. All this we ask in the goddess's name."*

I must shield Zac from the onslaught of magic that erupts around us. I curl my body around his and I prepare to keep those I love alive as I throw up a cinderblock wall of magic separating us from them. The world goes black around Zac and me as I hug him tighter, refusing to let him go for any reason.

Chapter 15

"**S**he's not one of us."

"But you heard her call."

"I heard Lailah's call."

"Lailah is Fallen. She cannot call to us."

"Those are Lailah's wings."

"Impossible."

"I believe she's human."

"No, not human. She smells of amber and moss."

"Impossible."

"You keep saying that, but there she is."

"What do we do with her?"

"We may not interfere."

"But we must help if called."

"We must help our own."

"Isn't she one of us? Her wings are born of us and we can hear her call."

"Do those things truly make her one of our own?"

"Of course they do."

"We're not meant to help these creatures."

"She called to us."

"We may not interfere in their battle."

"She has our wings and we hear her call. How can you say that does not make her one of us?"

"This is all impossible."

"You really must stop saying that."

"We have to help her."

"How? What does she need from us?"

"I suppose we do need to find that out."

"Child, why did you call us?"

Are they talking to me now? And if so, who are they? It sounds like three different people are having this conversation. I've met the Witan now and they don't sound like any of them. And what do they mean I called to them? I wrap my arms more firmly around Zac's body. Slowly, I open my eyes. To darkness.

Where are we? What is wrapped around us? I shift, and whatever is covering us moves with me. It's not my magic that has formed a shield around us. It's something else. I shift my shoulders trying to remove it and a pinch in my back makes me stop. It didn't hurt exactly. It just feels heavy. I try again and it's easier this time, but it's still there, the heaviness pressing against me.

"See, she doesn't even know how to move them. She is not one of us."

"Give her a moment to get her bearings."

Closing my eyes for a second to build my strength and courage, I wrap my arms around Zac and stand up. As I do, light comes rushing in as whatever is shielding us falls behind me. Is that a feather in Zac's hair? It takes a second for my eyes to adjust to the light and when they do, I can very clearly see that it is a feather. Looking over my shoulder, my nose comes millimeters from bumping into a giant wing. I stumble forward to get away from whoever's wing it is, but it follows me. When I turn around to face it, it's behind me.

"What is she doing?"

"I don't know."

In my quest for the wing holder, I forgot about the voices for a second. Raising my eyes, I find three people standing about ten feet away from me and Zac. There's a man and two women. I'm fairly certain they're Angels. "Oh no, am I dead?"

"Of course not," the male Angel says.

Looking around me, everyone else is still here. Kallen has risen to his feet, Grandma is squared off against Maeva, and Mom is in Fatin's face. But none of them are moving. "Are they dead?" I ask.

"See, she doesn't know anything. She is not one of us." This is said by one of the most beautiful women I have ever seen. She has long, straight black hair. Her skin is a creamy caramel color, her eyes slanted ever so slightly like a cat's. She is wearing something like an Indian sari dyed in rich colors of red, blue, and purple. She looks like a Persian princess. A very annoyed Persian princess.

Taking in the other two, they are just as beautiful. The man has flawless skin the color of a rich mocha with dark hair that's cut short. He has an aquiline nose and a chiseled chin and cheek bones. His eyes are a deep brown and his full lips are smiling. He has on dark pants that hug his leg muscles but no shirt. The other woman has on a long flowing, pure white dress in an ancient Greek style. She has auburn hair and the most perfect complexion I have ever seen. Her skin looks like ivory and her pink lips make a natural bow that looks half a step away from smiling even when she's not.

"She can look upon us," the smiling man says. "That is proof enough she is one of us."

"No, child, they are not dead," the woman with the auburn hair finally answers my question.

"Then why aren't they moving?"

A sigh escapes the Persian princess. "We have taken you out of their time. You do not exist in their time when you are here, and here time moves differently. If we send you back, they will not even know you've been gone." If they send me back?

Wow, and I thought physics was hard to understand. All these time differences between realms are getting confusing. "Why did you take me out of my time?"

The woman with auburn hair walks towards me. "Let me take him for you, it has been a long time since I have held a child. Then we will explain."

I try not to frown as I decide whether I want to hand Zac over to this woman. Yes, she looks like an Angel, but this could also be an elaborate trick the Witan cooked up. Sensing my hesitation, she laughs and it's like a ray of sunshine on a stormy day. "I will not harm him. I simply love children."

The feeling that I am safe here washes over me and I hand Zac to her. She smiles and begins to softly sing him a lullaby as she walks a few steps away, rocking him gently. He has not woken up yet. I really hope he's okay.

"Are you Angels?" I ask. Okay, so the wings are a dead giveaway, but I still want to be sure.

The man nods his head. "We are. The question now is – what are you?"

That's an easy question. "I'm half Witch and half Fairy."

"Impossible," the woman with long black hair says. "Witches and Fairies cannot mate. It would be like a lion and a tiger mating. It simply is not done in nature."

Does she have to talk about it as mating? "My father is a Fairy and my mother is a Witch. There's even a prophecy about it."

The Angel holding Zac looks up. "Prophecy?" She turns excitedly to the other Angels. "Has the prophecy come about then, Urim?"

The male Angel inclines his head. "Indeed, it has."

"Finally, I've been waiting so long for you! Urim was very naughty not telling us the prophecy is coming to fruition."

I'm not sure we're talking about the same prophecy. In the one I know the Angels are crying. "Are you talking about the prophecy where I destroy the world?"

"Silly girl, you don't..."

"Valoel, you mustn't," the other female Angel says. "You could change the course of things."

Valoel's bottom lip pushes out ever so slightly. I didn't know Angels pouted. "But she has it all wrong, Tabbris."

"She has been given enough information to make her choices, and they need to be her choices," Tabbris says. With her black hair and green eyes, she could be Kallen's sister. Even her personality seems a bit like his.

"Oh, pah," Valoel says waving a hand as if to say it doesn't matter. "She asked for help so that means we need to help her. Look around you, Tabbris. She is in the middle of a magical war, the likes of which hasn't been seen in millennia. It is time for us to step in."

"Peace cannot exist everywhere, Valoel. She must choose her own way." Tabbris' voice has a finality to it that causes Valoel's lip to extend a tiny bit farther out.

Urim finally joins the conversation again. "It is her fate to find us. She is to draw strength and power from us."

Tabbris' face sets like stone. "I don't like this, Urim."

He inclines his heads in empathy. "I understand."

"Um, I hate to interrupt, but could one of you tell me what's going on? Why do I have wings on my back?"

"I would like to know the answer to that myself," Tabbris says. Her facial expression hasn't changed, but it is amazing how she can look beautiful and annoyed at the same time. I thought Angels were supposed to be nice and happy?

"I believe the explanations fall to you, Urim," Voloel says and she rubs her nose against Zac's. He'd be dying of embarrassment if he was awake right now. Pushing that thought aside, I turn my attention back to Urim. Kallen is gorgeous but there aren't words to describe how handsome Urim is.

"So it does, Vol." Looking at me, he says, "I suppose I should start from the beginning." Oh, I bet this is going to be a really long story.

"Don't worry, it's a good story," Voloel says as if she had read my mind and earning her a snarky look from Tabbris. "But perhaps the beginning should include introductions. My name is Voloel, and I am the Angel of Peace. Tabbris is the Angel of Self-determination; she helps maintain free will. Urim is the Angel of Illumination and it falls to him to determine our fates. We must all work together, you see, a system of checks and balances, you could say, to keep the realms of sentient beings habitable. There is a fourth, Lailah, the Angel of Love and Conception, but she is fallen right now."

Okay, there are a couple of things I don't understand in those introductions. "What do you mean by habitable?"

"Sentient beings tend to be a bit volatile," she says diplomatically.

I think I know what she means. "We fight and go to war a lot."

Her long auburn hair is pushed back and to the side now, so it's no longer draping over Zac's still sleeping head. Even her ears are pretty. "That is part of it, yes, but there's more. Sentient beings have a wide range of emotions and even the good ones can have devastating effects on the realms. As Angels, we can sometimes whisper encouragement, help steer people in the right direction, but we may not impose our will. Tabbris is quite effective at keeping us in line. I believe her job is the most difficult." She gives Tabbris an affectionate look and the hint of a smile forms on the other Angel's lips.

"But there have been times we've had to exert some control, or ask the aid of other beings, to save humanity from destruction. Only when the need is dire may we interfere," Tabbris says. I think Voloel has softened her up a bit now.

This is interesting, but it's not really helpful for my current situation. "Okay, I get what you guys do, but why do I have wings? I'm not an Angel, and what did you mean when you said Lailah is 'Fallen?'"

Urim jumps back into the discussion with a dazzling grin. "Patience, young one, we are old beings and have much time on our hands to enjoy telling our stories." Great, even the Angels think I'm impatient. They may have all the time in the world, or universe, but I don't. I feel like I'm aging right now.

"Angels, of course, have been around since the beginning of time," Urim continues. "Over the years, new beings were brought into existence and it is our job to watch over them as Voloel has explained."

"Just watch them." Tabbris gives him a pointed look but he ignores her.

"As I was saying, it is our job to watch over them and we have done this in many ways over the millennia. Unfortunately, humans began to ignore our guidance. They began to seek power and wealth; and the harmony among many of them quickly disintegrated. Yet, there were pockets, here and there, of people who wanted to be led in a better direction. It was because of them that we would Fall."

"What do you mean?" I ask trying hard to sound patient.

"We would become Fallen Angels. We would assume a human form, in a toned-down version of ourselves, of course."

"Why a toned-down version?"

"Because to look at us in our natural state, as you are now, will cause blindness in humans, Witches, Fairies and most other beings."

I still don't get it. "Then why aren't you blinding me?"

"I will get to that soon enough, impatient one. When Angels Fall, we become like Witches. We retain some of our abilities, some of our magic. In the past, we would become priests and priestesses, teaching humankind how to survive in peace. We used our magic to protect them until they reached a point where they could defend themselves from magical beings."

"So, you were born knowing you were an Angel?"

Urim shakes his head. "No, when we Fall, we are what you consider adults. There are legends in your realm of the priests and priestesses who appeared from the mist fully grown."

I crinkle my brow. "Like the druids in King Arthur's time?"

He smiles. "Yes, we have often been referred to as druids, among other names."

"Are there a lot of Angels who have Fallen?"

"No. Sadly, there came a point where too many humans simply stopped listening to us. We may still Fall for personal reasons, but most of us choose not to anymore."

"Why?"

"When we are Fallen, we age as humans do and live out a human life. So, even though we start as adults, we still may live sixty or seventy years in our human form. That time is a blink of the eye for us when we are here in our realm, but the time passes slowly for us on earth. That is a long time to live with no one listening to you."

"Then why did the Angel who Voloel was talking about Fall?"

Voloel answers and for the first time since I arrived here, she looks sad. "Our Angel of Love wanted to experience human love for herself. Regrettably, it has not turned out well for her."

"Then can't she just come back?" It seems like that would be a perk of being an Angel.

"No," Tabbris says and she looks sad, as well. "Once the choice is made to Fall, we must live out our human life until death. We must make choices as a human would. And if we choose poorly, we cannot return to our Angel form. Lailah is dangerously close to that."

"You keep saying human, but you said you have the powers of a Witch when you're Fallen."

Voloel waves her hand in the air as if to say it doesn't matter. "Oh, that's just semantics. Witches, Fairies, humans. You are all humanoid; you all start from the same pattern. Some of you are simply more magical than others."

That makes sense, I guess. "Did she know who she wanted to fall in love with?" I can't help myself, I'm curious.

Tabbris is back to looking angry again. "She did. I warned her that his mind was weak, easily controlled by others, but she Fell anyway. If she had listened to me, she would not be in the mess she is in."

I don't know if I want to pursue this topic anymore. Not if Tabbris is this upset about it. I'd hate to be her scapegoat. "I'm afraid I still don't understand why I can be in your presence without being blinded."

Voloel raises her eyes to mine. "Because you have the blood of an Angel, of course."

Um, I don't think so. "I really think you have me confused with someone else. Like I said, my biological father is a Fairy and my mom is a Witch."

Urim says gently, as if I'm a child, "As I am the Angel of Fates, it is important I keep track of who is who. Your Angel blood did not originate with your parents."

Okay, he lost me again. "Then who?"

"Your grandmother is a Fallen Angel. She is Lailah, but that is not the name she goes by in your realm."

I'm quite sure my mouth has dropped so far open that they have a clear view of my tonsils. Maybe even my esophagus. "Grandma. Grandma is an Angel."

Urim inclines his head in confirmation. "A Fallen Angel, yes."

So, that means it was *Grandpa* she Fell for? Literally. Wow, she did choose badly. "My grandma is the Angel of Love."

Urim nods. "The Angel of Love and Conception. It was her blood which allowed the conception to occur between your mother and your father."

Great. Thanks, Grandma. "So, when you guys Fall, you can have babies and all that?" Not that I'm a prude, but I kinda thought Angels were virginal.

Urim laughs. "We can enjoy the pleasures of the skin if we find ourselves in love, but no, Angels do not have children when they Fall. Your mother and you are unique."

That's a nice way of saying that we're freaks of nature, I think.

"So, Grandma hasn't had any other kids over the millennia?"

Voloel shakes her head. "This is the first time Lailah has Fallen."

"Ever?" I ask in shock. "And she chose *Grandpa*?"

"Yes," Tabbris says. Her face is stony again. "She could not be talked out of it." I have the impression Tabbris did a lot of talking on the subject.

"In her defense, he was a lovely man when he was young. They were happy for a number of years," Voloel says.

Okay, I can't think about this anymore. "Why are you glad the prophecy is coming true? Do you want the world destroyed?" I've read stories that said Angels hate humans. Maybe they really do.

Voloel laughs her pretty laugh again. "You are not going to destroy the world; you are going to save it."

"I don't think so. The prophecy pretty clearly says that I'm going to destroy it."

"Humans have been misinterpreting prophecies from the beginning of time. I believe something gets lost in translation."

"Really?"

"Yes. Why don't you take us through line by line of the prophecy as it was explained to you, and then we will clear up any misconceptions you may have."

It would be great if I'm not destined to destroy the world. Maybe Grandpa and his awful friends will leave me alone. "The first line is 'a Witch's child of Fae is born when spirits of the realms are torn.'"

Urim nods. "Yes, that is true. The realms have been torn for quite some time. The Fairies, Witches and Humans have long been unable to live in harmony."

"This next part is what I've been talking about. 'Into the world, destruction she brings, while children cry and Angels sing.' Doesn't that mean I'm going to destroy the world and you guys are going to be happy about it?"

Voloel shakes her head. "No, of course not," she admonishes gently. "We love your world. The destruction you will bring will be to the way things are *now*. You will bring about change, not true destruction. As for the children crying, that is meta-phorical, not actual children. You are a tool to bring about the maturity of your people, and they will cry tears of joy when released from the bonds of their immaturity. They will stop behaving as children and learn to live peaceably together. That will be the reason we will sing."

Great. That sounds impossible. I still think they have the wrong person. "I'm going to bring about world peace?"

"Alas, as much as I would like that, no. As I said before, humans are much too volatile. But you will usher in a new age between Witches and Fairies. An age of peace and harmony."

"Um, my dad's pretty mad at humans and Witches. I don't see him being on board with this whole idea."

A sly smile touches Urim's lips. "You will find a way to make the changes."

I'm glad he has that much confidence in me because I don't. This sounds impossible for one person. Especially if that person is me. Instead of arguing, I'm just going to skip ahead. "The next part is 'none may survive the vengeance of she'. Doesn't that mean I get pretty violent? I hate to think that because I don't feel I could actually kill anybody."

"Think of it as more of a warning to others," Urim says. "You are a powerful being, even if your control is slightly erratic at present. You are not one to be challenged, for your magic is great."

Slightly erratic? Apparently, he hasn't been watching me very carefully. "So, I'm not actually going to take vengeance on people? It's just warning them that if they cross me, I *could* take vengeance on them?"

Tabbris answers this time. "There will be times when you are faced with difficult choices and you will have to decide which path to follow. But you are not *required* to take vengeance on anyone."

Well, that's a relief. I'm really curious about the next part. I've been kind of ignoring it because I don't think it's possible. "What about when it says, 'immortal her soul is to be, to remedy the world of its natural discord'?"

"Ah, immortality, the quest of many, but found by a precious few," Urim says and he sounds wistful.

"So, I'm not going to be immortal?"

Voloel lifts her head as she brushes Zac's hair from his forehead. "That will be up to you."

"What?"

Her smile becomes bright again. "If you fulfill the prophecy, your soul will be immortal. Immortality comes in different forms, though."

Tabbris looks at Voloel and says, "I'm afraid we mustn't say anything else on the subject." Voloel gives her a slight nod in agreement.

"I really appreciate you telling me all this, but I still don't know how I called you or what I'm supposed to do about this." I sweep my hand in the direction of the statue-like people in my drive-way.

"When an Angel is in trouble, his or her wings call for help," Voloel explains.

That's kind of cool. "Speaking of these wings, am I going to have them all the time now?"

"I suspect not," Urim says but he doesn't sound sure. "Since you did not have them before, it would seem they only come to you when you are in dire straits."

I'm okay with that. I'd hate to have to try and sleep with these things on. How do the Angels do it? "They'll come to protect me if I need them?"

He nods. "Yes, they are to serve you in such a manner."

"Can I fly with them?"

He chuckles and his laugh is as beautiful as Voloel's. "Yes, you can fly, but only when you have your wings."

"Will you come every time my wings come to me?"

"No," he says, "Unless your wings send us a distress call. They will do this if you are truly in need of assistance, but they will do their best to protect you without additional help."

"So, I was in danger of being seriously hurt out here?" I gesture again towards the scene in the driveway.

His full lips purse for a second. "I don't believe so. I think your wings called to us so we could explain their purpose."

Oh, that's disappointing. I was kind of hoping they'd be guiding me on this quest for peace I'm supposed to be on. "So, what do I do now?"

Tabbris gives me her first real smile. "That is the beauty of free will. You will choose how you handle this."

I don't think I like free will a whole lot at the moment. "Will you guys be watching to make sure I do it right?"

"We will check in on you from time to time," Urim says, "but this is a battle you must face alone."

"Will Zac be okay?"

"He is fine," Voloel assures me. "He will awaken as soon as you return. I have kept him still while you've been here so as not to damage his eyes."

Oh, that's why she was so eager to hold him. Though, I do think part of it was because she genuinely loves children. "Thank you."

"We must be going now," Tabbris says and the tone of her voice suggests the other two shouldn't argue.

"Can I ask one more question?"

"Certainly," Voleol says.

"I'm pretty sure Kallen knows that Grandma is a Fallen Angel. How would he know that?" I'm assuming they don't go around announcing that they're Fallen Angels when they're in our realms.

Tabbris answers me. "As I mentioned, there have been times we have asked other magical creatures for assistance in helping the humans. The Sheehogue Fairies have been among those. We have a pact with them that they will do their best to help humans on our behalf, but this agreement states that they will not impose their wills upon humans, either. Nor may they cause unnecessary harm to other humans, Fairies, or Witches. In return, we have made them more powerful than their counterparts in order to follow through with their agreement."

"So, they're more powerful than the Pooka Fairies because of you."

"Yes. They are also sworn to secrecy concerning our existence and the magic we have extended to them. If they make it known that we have this pact, they will lose their magic completely." Oh, that explains why Kallen didn't say anything. Yeah, I would have kept my mouth shut, too. Looking at Urim and Voloel, Tabbris says, "We really must be going."

"Can I ask one more question?"

Tabbris is annoyed again but she says, "One more."

"Is it because Mom's part Angel that she's been able to hold her and Dad in our realm?"

Voloel answers. "Oh, silly girl, you are holding them in your realm, not your mother."

Quite sure they can see my tonsils again. "I'm holding them here?"

She nods. "Yes. Even though your mother has Angel blood, she is still not strong enough to hold them both. It is the powerful mixture within you which makes it possible for them to exist as they are. Spirits who remain are not usually the same as they were in life."

I'm half proud and half terrified. "Is it okay I'm doing that?"

"As long as it is what they desire," Tabbris says. "Right now, it is their choice to remain. When the time comes that they are ready to move on, you will have to release them. If you don't, you will be taking away their free will." I suspect she would have something to say about it if that happened. "Because your hold on them is so strong, you are the only one who can release them to what lies beyond," she says meaningfully. "Now, there is no more time for questions."

Urim nods in acknowledgement. "Then we shall take our leave." Turning to me, he says, "Xandra, it has truly been a pleasure. I wish you the best and I know you will live up to the prophecy set before you."

I wish I was that sure. It still sounds like an impossible task. I can't see my biological father forgiving and forgetting, let alone agreeing to live in harmony. "How do I get back?"

"As soon as we leave, you will be returned to your realm and time."

I'm not sure if I'm ready but I guess I can't put it off forever. "Thanks for everything. I hope I see you again under better circumstances."

"As do we. Goodbye, Xandra." And then they're gone.

Chapter 16

Zac is back in my arms and I am back in my own realm and time. The fighting has stopped as everyone turns to stare at me and my new wings. Depending on whose eyes I meet, there is either awe or fear in them. Grandma seems the most surprised of all.

"What is going on?" Grandpa demands to no one in particular. "Where did those wings come from?"

"It doesn't matter, it's just more proof she's not meant to be," Maeva growls but her words don't get rid of the fear I've already seen in her eyes.

"Oh, shut up," I say and her mouth closes. She's making some weird mumbling noises, but she can no longer speak. Turning to Fatin, I say, "You will release my father."

His confidence from earlier shaken, but he rallies pretty well. "I hold the cards here. I am seconds away from sending him to the hereafter."

I roll my eyes. "Really? Because I'm the only one who can release him from this plane of existence, so your threat isn't really a threat. It's wishful thinking on your part."

Fatin obviously doesn't believe me because he begins to say the exorcism spell again. *"Spirit in unrest, soul in pain, come to me, find peace again. Leave this world of longing and woe, sorrow filled days no longer you'll know…"*

"Xandra, make him stop!" Mom cries.

"Mom, trust me. Nothing's going to happen."

"…your soul I release, and you shall rest in peace."

Like I said, nothing happens. Fatin is really ruffled now. He begins to say the spell again, more forcefully, *"Spirit in unrest, soul in pain…"*

"Oh, zip it." Now he's gagged as well.

"I demand to know where those wings came from!" Grandpa shouts at me.

I give him my sweetest smile. "That's nice. Thanks for sharing." I turn my back on him.

Grandma finds her voice and asks with a slight tremor, "Xandra, are you…" Her words trail off.

"Dead? Nope. I'm very much alive." Relief shows in the eyes of everyone on my side and disappointment in the rest. "As for you? You are not to do anything that will jeopardize your future." I'm pretty sure she knows what I mean because she gives me a slight nod, and then she visibly tries to subdue her anger with deep breaths and closed eyes.

"Athear, what is she talking about?" Grandpa practically growls. "Is she threatening you?"

I have to laugh at that. "The only ones here who are threatening her are you and your disgusting menagerie of followers. Though, if we're all going to be honest," I look each member of the Witan in the eye, "you are actually the follower, not the followed. I suspect your mind hasn't been your own for a long time." There is some slight shuffling of discomfort among the Witan.

"What nonsense is this? I'm King, of course my mind is my own."

I shake my head. "Think again. I bet every thought you have feels like it's been planted by someone else."

Grandpa looks like he's going to get all blustery again, but doubt is creeping over his face like a caterpillar, leaving its sticky little footprints all over him. Instead of speaking to me, he turns to Louhi. "Is this true?"

"Of course not," Louhi says indignantly.

I laugh. "As if you could be trusted to tell the truth. I doubt your twisted little mind even knows what that is anymore."

"I've heard enough out of you, little girl," he hisses. Oh, that's a sound that's going to haunt my nightmares. He should try his luck in Hollywood. I'm sure he'd get a lot of roles as a villain, and they wouldn't even have to put make up on him. "Say the spell again," he tells the others.

I shake my head. "It didn't work the first time, what makes you think it's going to work this time?"

"You are not omnipotent. You can be brought down and we're going to be the ones to do it."

"Okay. Go ahead then." I wave my hand in a hurry up gesture.

He's surprised. What, I'm supposed to be begging at his feet? I don't think so. "What?" he says.

I say my words slowly as if he's new to the English language. "O.

Kay. Go. A. Head. Then."

That earns a big-time glare from him and his eyes narrow into little slits like slots for demon coins. Could the man get any creepier looking? Forget I asked that, I really don't want to know.

As if following my thoughts, Louhi snarls, "A pair of demon wings doesn't scare us."

Hmm. I turn around to look at Kallen. "Do demons have wings?"

He shakes his head. "No, they do not."

"That's what I thought." Turning back to Louhi, I say, "Could you please keep your insults to things that really exist instead of making crap up?"

Wow, he's really pissed now. Between gritted teeth, he says to the others, "Say the spell again."

"Now hold up one minute. I want to give you guys a sporting chance."

"We have all the advantage we need."

"Oh, it's cute how you get so mean and tough when you're angry."

From behind me, Mom says quietly, "Xandra, be careful." Okay, maybe that was a bit much. I might be practically indestructible but no one else is. I don't need him taking his anger towards me out on my family or Kallen.

"Fine," I say. "Tell you what. I'm going to make this fair. It'll just be me and the eight of you. I won't ask anyone else for help." Except my wings, of course, but they're a part of me now.

Maeva looks at me for a long moment. "Why would you do such

a thing?"

I shrug. "It's not them you want, it's me. Right? I don't want them to get hurt in the crossfire."

"Xandra, I will not allow you to fight them alone." Kallen's voice is full of emotion and I turn to smile at him.

"I know it'll be hard for you, but it's for the best. I need to do this alone."

"Xandra, this is suicide," Mom says. "We are all going to fight right along next to you."

I look at her unyielding face for several heartbeats. "Mom, please."

She shakes her head. "No, we are staying right here with you."

I sigh heavily. What I'm about to do is going to make her really mad at me. I'll probably be grounded for a year. I close my eyes for just a second to collect my thoughts. When I open them, Kallen, Mom, Dad, Zac, Aunt Barb, and Grandma are being propelled backwards towards the house.

"Xandra, don't do this," Kallen says. "You don't have to do this alone." Wow, he can use contractions. Huh. Maybe it's only when he's mad.

"But I do," I whisper more to myself than him. When they are all safely in the house, I throw up a wall that divides the house from where I'm standing with the Witan. I know it's sturdy enough that neither side will be able to get through unless I take it down.

Now, it's time to deal with the Witan.

Chapter 17

"**Y**ou are a stupid child," Davina says speaking up for the first time. She has the look of pity about her. That's okay. If they expect little from me, they'll be even more surprised.

"It must take a lot of magic to keep such a wall in place," Midar says. He lumbers up next to Maeva after finally leaving his spot behind one of the cars where he has been hiding.

I shrug. "Not really."

His eyebrows rise in skepticism. "We are all experienced Witches. We know better than you the amount of magic things like that," he points at my wall, "take."

I offer him a simpering expression. "You know how much it takes of *your* magic, not mine."

Maeva waves her hand in the air as if to brush away my comment. "Magic is magic."

"True," I acknowledge. "But the power behind it is what's most important."

Louhi sneers at me. "You believe your power to wield magic is greater than ours? All eight of us combined? The world will be a better place with one less fool in it."

Hey, he just called me a fool. That's not very nice. Though, I guess it's better than some of the names that have been going through my head for him. "Can we just get on with this? I could use a nice hot shower. Here, I'll even take off all these talismans and amulets." Anything to hurry this along. My clothes are still a little wet and cold and I don't have a coat on.

Beren's eyebrows are nearly at his hairline. "Are you that confident or that eager to die?"

I pretend to think about it a minute. "I'm going to go with confident."

Grandpa's standing off to the side now looking a bit befuddled. He keeps glancing at these people who are supposed to be his most trusted council and friends. The seed of doubt I planted in his head seems to have taken root. I don't think he knows whose side he's on now.

"I'll tell you what else I'm going to do. Let's take turns. You guys do a spell and then I do one, kind of like Russian roulette." The Witan look at each other. The thought 'she's crazy' is going through all their minds.

Finally, Fatin shrugs. "As the saying goes, it is your funeral. Shall we speak the spell again?" he asks the others. He gets several curt nods. I notice he didn't get one from Grandpa.

Seven voices ring out clearly as they say the spell to kill me again. Grandpa stays quiet. *"From ancient times of rhymes and runes, these witches call upon the power of the moon to scourge the earth of magic black, and within its womb to take mercifully back, this one born in heresy and shame, and those who've shielded her also to blame, swallow their guilt and show us their pain. All this we ask in the goddess's name."*

I count to ten and then say, "My turn?"

There are a couple of nervous glances exchanged before Louhi collects himself from the shock of me still standing and sneers, "Go ahead. We can take whatever you dish out."

And they think I'm cocky? "I'm afraid I'm not very good with spells, so you'll have to bear with me as I do my own thing, okay?" Louhi laughs cruelly.

Oh, he is so my first target. Pulling magic from the earth, I barely have time to feel it inside of me before I'm pushing it out. Half a millisecond later, Louhi is on his knees gasping in pain.

"What are you doing to him?" Davina demands.

"Significantly less than what you want to do to me," I say acerbically.

"Let him go and I'll take my turn," Midar says in that fake English accent. He sounds so stupid. Why haven't his friends ever told him that? Then again, he doesn't seem like the type who would listen, anyway.

I shrug. "Okay." I pull back my magic and Louhi falls forward, catching himself with his hands before he goes face first into the snow. He looks like he's about to have a heart attack. He glowers up at me as he tries to get his breathing under control.

"There is no hope, only sorrow. Blackness fills your every tomorrow. This life of yours isn't worth living, if you always take but are never giving. Put an end to the misery and pain, the circle of life comes around again. Each day will be a trip through hell under this Witch's darkness spell, until at last, you can take no more, then end your days miserable and poor."

As the magic from his spell comes toward me, wanting to wrap me in its dark cocoon, my wings shift. They fan out to the sides as far as they can, and then gently begin to curve in, creating a sort of shield. Apparently, it's a good shield because Midar's magic, which I can barely see, stops its forward progression. In a flash, it's heading back towards him, too fast for him to shield himself or form a circle. As it hits him, his rotund body slips to the ground in a heap, his eyes become unfocused and he begins to drool. It's really hard to look at the pathetic mess he's just become as he finally gets a taste of his own magic.

Now he's crying so hard a big stream of snot is coming out his nose. "Can we throw a blanket over him or something? That's disgusting!"

Fatin cringes when he looks at him and then turns away in repulsion. "He has always been a weak mind." Gee, I thought all these guys liked each other.

I drag my eyes from the blob that is Midar. "My turn?"

Fatin waves a hand in front of him in a 'be my guest' gesture. Now I'm torn, other than Louhi, who I abhor, I hate the rest of them the same. So, who do I go for now?

"Today would be nice," Maeva says snidely. Well, that settles my dilemma.

"Alright, maybe I will try my hand at a spell. I do need the practice and I've only blown up the house twice today. You don't mind, Maeva, do you? Third time's a charm, right?" A vein on the side of her head starts to spasm as if all her blood is rushing to her head to try to convince her to run. Her eyes dart back and forth to her cohorts, probably looking for a sign they're going to come to her aid. They don't. Weasels. They don't care about each other, only themselves.

The words for a spell pop into my head like they've been eagerly waiting for me to call on them. I wonder if my wings are feeding them to me. "It's a simple spell, but we all have to start small, right?" I give her a sweet smile and I walk towards her. She looks nervous but she holds her ground, even when I lay my hand on her shoulder. "You tell me if I get this right, okay?" I drag my finger across her shoulder and back as I walk around her in a circle. *"Identities stolen, wrong skin worn, built from trickery and unchecked scorn. Strip away these magical lies; never again deceive one's eyes. Magic abused, power out of control, I strip these now from your wicked soul. Witch no more shall you be, no spells, no evil trickery. Your magic has been set free."*

Maeva's arms spread out to the side. Her eyes roll back, and her face looks towards the sky. A silent scream is torn from her as all her magical abilities are scrubbed out of her, down to her very DNA. It looks really, really painful. Glad I'm on the casting side of the spell and not the receiving side. On a positive note, I didn't blow her up.

Davina gasps and rushes to Maeva's side as her silent screams are shouted to the sky. When the very last soundless syllable is stolen from her mouth, she collapses into the other woman's arms. I think she's unconscious. Beren opens one of the car doors and helps Davina lay Maeva on the back seat.

A woman who's been standing back towards the trees walks forward. I know who she is even though she's kept her face hidden from me. I've seen her work. She's the one who made the ugly doll that was supposed to be me. Maybe she should have taken a few sculpture classes over the years.

"Perhaps a different kind of magic is called for," she says. From her coat pocket she pulls out a small doll. Yup, it's just as ugly as the first one. Really, just one class probably would have helped. She pulls a lighter from her pocket, one of those old silver ones that you need to put lighter fluid in and holds the flame to the doll. I refuse to say likeness because it looks nothing like me. *"I melt this wax as I melt your will. Child of darkness, your body be still. I bind these hands as I bind thee, a force unbreakable ties you to me.*

Cast aside your desires, consumed by my fire, as I control your mind and bring justice to our time. As I beckon, come to me, your will is no longer free."

I double over and stumble towards her, as if pulled by a rope that I'm trying to frantically free myself from. I see the victory in her eyes as I move ever closer to her, one hand on my stomach, the other in front of me as if to stop the power of her spell. I glance at the others who are practically jumping for joy at Annika's success.

I must walk around both cars to get to her since she tried to keep herself safe by hiding behind them when magic was flying. She and Midar are a matched set in the bravery department, apparently. When I am directly in front of her, I stand up and I snatch the doll out of her hand. The look on her face was worth the minute and a half of pretending to be beaten by this worthless bunch.

Giving my new wings a try, I think about where I want to be and next thing I know, I'm flying there. I'm back to where I was standing before. This is so cool but I'm a bit wobbly. I hope I have them long enough today to practice some more. I wonder how high I can go.

Giving Annika a smug smile, I say, "Don't feel bad. Grandpa tried that spell on me earlier and it didn't work for him either. But now it's my turn again." I tap a finger of the hand not holding the doll against my chin. "What shall I do?"

There are six Witches standing in front of me now who are a whole lot less confidant than they were fifteen minutes ago. At the back of my brain, I can feel Kallen, Grandma and Mom joining forces to try to free themselves from the magic I'm using to keep them locked in the house. It's not going to work. The added power I feel because of my wings makes me stronger than all three of them put together.

"I know!" I say brightly which causes Annika to jump, which makes me laugh. Turning to Louhi, I say, "Your theory as to why you have become this," I wave my hand up and down to indicate I mean all of him, "is because of all those minds you are carrying around with you. I think you're right. I can't imagine you always looked like this. I know we're not supposed to judge people by their appearance, but you must scare small children with that face. Hmm," I say as I tap my chin again, "I'll have to ask Zac when he wakes up. But anyway, I'm going to help you out with that. Free up some clutter."

These ideas are jumping into my head from nowhere and as soon as I think it, I know I can do it. I think the Angels held a little information back about these wings. I think they not only protect me but guide me as well. Not that I mind. I'm so new to this stuff, I can use the help.

I close my eyes, and I'm fairly certain Louhi is growling at me. I can see him in my mind's eye with his skinny little lips pulled up in a snarl like a rabid poodle. A rabid, bald poodle. Trying to ignore the disturbing image, I send my magic out on its mission. I feel it when it hits Louhi's protection circle, and I feel it when it crumbles the circle like it's nothing more than a cobweb in a dusty corner. Now I'm in his mind and it's just as dark and twisted as I thought it would be.

It seems he has been able to portion his mind off into sections. There are dark pockets that are closed off from other parts of his mind. It's in these pockets where he keeps the minds he has stolen from others. Like a thief, I pick the locks and creep quietly inside these foreboding closets. When I open them to the light, bolts of lightning spark around me as these minds awaken from their long slumber. Louhi has quite a collection in here. Most of these minds I can tell are innocent; incarcerated and lobotomized because their opinions differed from those of the Witan.

A couple of the minds truly came from those who committed crimes and were probably rightfully imprisoned. One committed murder and other unspeakable things, while another was abusive to his family and paralyzed his daughter. I let Louhi keep these minds as I set the others free. I lock the doors behind me so no one can get out, or in, and I pull myself from his mind.

When I open my eyes again, Louhi is holding his head like he's trying to keep those minds in place. But it's too late. They've already escaped back to their rightful places, never to see the inside of Louhi's mind again.

"Get her," Louhi growls. But the murderous expression he still wears is no longer mirrored on the other Witch's faces. They are finally starting to see this is a fight they may not win.

"It *is* your turn," I encourage.

No one says anything. They exchange some nervous looks, but no one steps up and says, 'my turn.' Well, I'm not going to wait all day for them. I'm cold. Sensing my discomfort, my wings fold over my shoulders, giving me their warmth. "If you aren't going to take your turn, can I go again to speed this along? I'm craving a cup of hot chocolate big time."

Now they're even more nervous. I could probably get away with saying scared. Even Fatin, so jovial in his cockiness earlier, is ruffled. "Oh, this is ridiculous," I say, losing my patience. Turning to Grandpa, I say, *"Release this man from his bonds. His mind is now his own."* Okay, it doesn't rhyme, but I'm certain I got my point across to the magic.

Grandpa's eyes that have looked a little glazed over every time I've seen him become suddenly clear. It only takes him a second to realize what happened. His eyes are flashing hot with anger now as he rounds on his Witan. "You! I trusted you. All of you. Yet you have been preying on my anguished mind all these years! Turning me from a King to nothing more than a mere puppet! Turning me against my wife and my daughter, and my granddaughter!"

It's nice of him to throw me in there at the end, sort of like an afterthought. Turning towards me, he says, "My dear, I don't know if you can ever forgive me, but I give you my word, I would not have done and said the things I have if it were not for the hold they had on me."

I look at him with skeptical eyes. "Yeah, I'm not feeling the warm and fuzzies from that speech. Maybe you can try your luck with Grandma." Fat chance of that either. She Fell for him and her life for the last eighteen years has sucked royally.

Grandpa looks sad. I still don't believe his miraculous recovery is all legitimate, but I do feel sorry for him. He's lost his family and his friends now. Looking a little lost, he says, "Where do we go from here?"

I raise my brows. "Is that your subtle way of saying you don't want to kill me anymore?"

Shame washes over his face. "I never truly wanted to kill you."

Yeah, right. "Look, save it, okay? I'm cold and frankly, I'm tired of talking to the lot of you. I want to go inside. So, the quicker I get rid of you, the better."

He nods. "I understand." Turning to the members of the Witan, he says, "This ends now. You will not do anything to harm my grandchild. As your King, I decree it to be so." He looks each of them in the eye and they nod in agreement. Turning back to me, he says, "We will leave you in peace now."

"Hold on a moment. You may be done, but I'm not. You and your lackeys have been abusing your power for a long time. I felt the minds that I released from Louhi's grasp, and most of them were unfairly judged. I'm not going to let you go off and do the same thing to others."

Grandpa's chest puffs out and his buttons must hold on for dear life. I can almost hear their tiny little pleas for him to exhale before they pop off into the snow. "I am still King, young lady."

Putting my fingers and thumb together, I cut him off. Literally. While he's trying to get his mouth open, I say, "Whether or not you remain King is yet to be determined. You can bluster and spout off as loudly as you want, but only real change is going to allow you to remain in your current position." I release the spell on Grandpa's mouth, but he stays quiet. I can tell he really wants to say something but he's smart enough to hold his tongue.

The rest of them are dead quiet, hanging on my every word. I've already stripped Maeva and Louhi of their power, and Midar is a snot covered mess trapped by his own magic. I'm assuming the others are hoping that if they stay quiet, I'll forget about them. Not likely.

I start with Annika. She's done the best job of keeping a low profile around me, only stepping out of the shadows that one time. Looking her dead in the eye, I say, "The ability to hurt someone from a distance with an ugly little doll is cowardly, not to mention annoying. Have you ever thought of getting some art education under your belt to make your likenesses more like actual likenesses?" She looks baffled, not sure if that was a rhetorical question or not. It wasn't but I continue anyway. "There is no need for such magic other than to dish out cruelty on others without actually having to look them in the eye when you do it. My gift to you is a nudge towards improving your character through social interaction instead of hiding behind your wax dolls. Or cars," I say, and I can't help a small giggle at her indignant face.

"I was not hiding behind the cars. I was waiting for the opportune moment to show my cards."

Uh huh. *"From plant to wax your tool of choice, I take from you your artistic voice."* What there is of it, anyway. *"Likenesses made to cause fear and pain, from your hands made never again."* My spells just aren't as catchy as some of the others I've read. I'll have to work on that.

Annika looks down at her hands in shock and then back up at me. "What have you done?"

I try to think of a nice way to put it, but I can't. "I guess you could say I neutered you. You can still perform some magic, just not Sympathetic magic." She is furious but she must be biting her tongue because she doesn't say anything.

"Xandra, I will not tolerate you treating these people like this. They may have wronged you, and me, but it is my right as King to decide their punishment." So, Grandpa got his groove back, huh? Yeah, that was cheesy even in my own head.

"Remember when I said that you remaining King is conditional? This is one of the conditions. I will not let these Witches go back and keep doing what they've been doing. If you don't like it, do something about it." I've thrown my challenge at his feet and I'm curious to see what he does with it.

Nothing. He clamps his lips together and tries not to glower at me. He doesn't succeed. I shake my head and turn away from him to size up Fatin for a long moment; long enough for him to start to squirm a little under the scrutiny. "What you do is not necessarily a terrible thing. If spirits stick around just to cause trouble, someone must help them pass on. I'm told that it's unusual for spirits to remain themselves like my mom and dad have, so I hate to admit it, but I don't think I should neuter you."

An uncomfortable and awkward moment hangs in front of us as we both take in what I just said. Eew. "Anyway, I need your word that you will only use your power for good." Again with the cheese. I might as well add 'and may the force be with you.' "Do I have your word?" Not that his word really means anything to me.

He hesitates just long enough for me to feel the need to add, "I will find out if you're doing something you're not supposed to do."

Like Grandpa, he looks like he wants to say something but instead, he pastes a fake smile on his face. "The extent of your wrath has been made perfectly clear. As a Witch who wishes to remain…intact, I agree to your conditions."

I kind of believe him so I move on to Beren and Davina. I think of them as a set. They seem to spend a lot of time together; I wonder if they're dating. "The same goes for the two of you. If Witches go bad, someone has to be able to apprehend them and bring them in." What, am I a cop now using their lingo? Moving on. "Will you agree to the same conditions as Fatin?"

There's no hesitation on their part. They say 'yes' right away. Something tells me they usually just go along with the flow of things. Regardless, I'm convinced they mean it. As much as they can, anyway.

I check them off in my head. Maeva can't become anything she's not or do anything else with magic. Louhi can't steal minds anymore. He doesn't know it yet, but he can't do any other type of magic, either. I think I'll leave that as a surprise. Midar is just useless at this point. Annika can't do sympathetic magic, the only magic she can do well. I don't know why I know that, but I do. I love these wings. Fatin, Davina, and Beren have agreed to change their wicked ways.

Grandpa's a little more difficult. He has been mind-controlled for such a long time. What if he doesn't know *how* to think on his own anymore? I'm going to need some help deciding this one.

I make a shooing gesture with my hand towards the others. "Go. Go home. At least, go away." Turning to Grandpa, I say, "You stay."

The others look at me, then at each other, and then at me again trying to figure out if they really can leave. "Go!" I say more forcefully.

They don't wait any longer. They walk towards the cars and I notice they don't stop to pick up Midar. "Uh uh, you are not leaving him here." Reluctantly, Fatin and Beren come back and after a couple of minutes of struggling with Midar's incredible body weight, they are finally able to shove him into the back seat of one of the cars. I think they did a quick game of rock, paper, scissors to determine who must drive that car and listen to the agony of depression dribbling from Midar's mouth.

After they are in their cars and backing out of their driveway, I turn to Grandpa again. "Come with me." He doesn't question me; he follows me towards the house where I'm going to let Grandma decide his fate. It seems only fair.

Chapter 18

W hen I bring down the wall, four extremely angry people are waiting for me. Mom and Dad look angrier than I've ever seen them before. Kallen looks like he may never speak to me again. Grandma, on the other hand, looks like she's a lot angrier with Grandpa than me if the death rays shooting from her eyes mean anything.

Zac definitely isn't mad at me. "Xan, you have wings! That is awesome. Where'd you get them?? Can I get some, too?"

I'm charmed by his excitement and I swoop down and give him a hug which he squirms out of as soon as he can. Mussing his hair, I say, "Sorry, buddy. No wings for you." Though he does have Angel blood running through his veins too, so maybe someday.

"Ah, that sucks. You get all the cool stuff."

"Yeah, but I get all the mean people coming after me, too."

"Uh uh, not just you. Aunt Barb and I got kidnapped today." He says it like it's the coolest thing in the entire world.

"Xandra, we need to talk to you," Mom says through a jaw clenched so hard I can barely make out her words. The look on her face gets her meaning across in a decidedly efficient way, though.

"Um, Zac, I have to talk to Mom and Dad for a few minutes. Can you go play in your room for a little while?"

He looks like he wants to argue until he sees Mom's face. He's a smart boy. He makes himself scarce fast.

"So, should I sit down, or do you guys want to kill me standing up?"

"Not funny," Dad says. Arms crossed over his chest, the expression on his face is about ten times angrier than the first time he saw Kallen and me kissing. Dad is officially a sociopath now, I think. I wonder if there's a cure. It's not like ghosts can take antipsychotic drugs.

"Kitchen. Now," Mom says, but since her jaw is no less tense than it was a minute ago, it comes out as 'itchen ow.'

"You sit," Grandma says to Grandpa. "We'll deal with you in a minute." He starts to speak but Grandma holds up her hand to stop him. "Save it." Just like Zac, he knows when not to argue. He sits down on the couch without saying a word. Grandma turns to follow Mom and Dad into the kitchen.

I pull my bottom lip through my teeth as I look at Kallen. His green eyes are sparking in fury, and underneath that, hurt. "I'm sorry," I mouth but he doesn't even acknowledge it. He turns and follows the others into the kitchen without a backwards glance at me. With feet that feel like they're walking through a combination of cement and quicksand, I walk towards the jury who will decide my punishment. Ironic after I just so easily passed down my own on the Witan.

Mom is pacing the kitchen, not even noticing that she keeps going through a chair each time she passes the table. She stops when she sees me standing in the doorway. My wings are almost tall enough to touch the frame on top. It's amazing how I don't even notice them anymore. They already feel like a part of me.

I'll miss them when they're gone.

Dad's the first one to speak. In a voice he has never used with me before, he bites out, "Of all the selfish, irresponsible, egotistical, idiotic, reckless, arrogant, foolish things to do, what you did out there topped the list. And where the *hell* did those wings come from?!"

I'm stunned into silence for a moment by the amount of emotion he packed into those two sentences. So, Kallen answers him for me. "They are Angel wings."

Dad's head spins so far to look at Kallen that if he weren't a ghost, he probably would have broken his neck. "What are you talking about?"

Instead of answering Dad, he looks at Grandma. "I am assuming since the wings are out of the bag, I am not violating my oath." Grandma shakes her head solemnly. "Then perhaps this is a tale for you to tell."

Grandma looks like she'd rather eat fried grasshoppers dipped in liver sauce than tell the story. But she does. She explains who she is, why she Fell, and how miserable she truly has been over the last eighteen years. At least now I believe it's true.

Mom's in shock. "Angel. You're an Angel? And now Xandra's an Angel?"

"I – I don't quite know what Xandra is," Grandma admits.

"No, not technically," I say, and I explain the whole wing thing and how we had the prophecy all wrong. Relief is visible on all their faces when they hear that. I go on to tell them what I did with the Witan, and despite everything, Mom and Dad are proud of me. Aunt Barb is still in shock over the whole thing.

A lot of my parents' anger seems to have dissipated as the stories unfolded. I think I may get out of this without being grounded for life or anything like that. Kallen, however, still looks pretty murderous where he's standing with his arms crossed over his chest and his shoulder leaning against the far wall. I'm dreading talking to him, but it must be done.

"Um, Mom, Dad, would you mind if I talked to Kallen alone for a few minutes?"

Mom looks from me to Kallen and back again. "I think that would be a good idea."

Without a word, Kallen walks out of the kitchen and down the hall towards my bedroom. I don't think he's going to let me off as easily as my parents. Looking at Grandma, I say, "Grandpa's fate is up to you. You need to decide whether he should still be King or not. I was thinking that maybe the Witches need their Queen more than they need their King, since he's been led around like a kitten by his Witan. But I didn't know if you want the job or not. Your call. Whatever you decide is fine with me and I'll back you up."

Grandma sighs. "I'm not sure what I want to do with him right now."

"I am," Dad growls and there's a wicked glint in his eyes that tells me I really don't want to know what he's thinking.

Grandma gets up from her chair at the table. "I'll go get him."

I take that as my cue to go after Kallen. I walk down the hall and when I get to my room, I step in and close the door behind me. He's leaning his back against my dresser with one foot crossed in front of the other. His muscular arms again folded tightly across his chest.

I don't say anything because I'm not quite sure what to say. He doesn't have the same problem. "Are you trying to get me killed?"

That was not anywhere close to what I thought he was going to say. "What?"

"I asked – are you trying to get me killed?" His words are terse and his face unyielding. I still don't know what he's talking about, though.

I say the only thing that comes to mind. "No."

"Your actions belie the truth of that word."

Frustrated, I huff, "Will you please tell me what you're talking about?"

He pushes away from the dresser, but his arms remain crossed as he comes to a halt right in front of me, forcing me to look up at him. I still hate it when he does that. "You do recall I have taken a blood oath, do you not?"

My face folds into a deep frown. "Yeah, what does that have to do with anything?" Finally, my mind catches up with my mouth. "Oh."

"It is difficult to protect a life as if it's my own when I am locked in a house by the magic of the person I am supposed to be protecting."

"So, even if I don't need your help, under the oath you still have to try to protect me or you could die." He gives me a 'now you got it' look. "Did I mention that I'm sorry?"

"No, I do not believe you have." Actually, I did mouth it to him, but I guess it doesn't really count if you don't say it out loud.

"Do you hate me now?"

His brows slam together in a scowl. "Is your world so black and white that I must either love you or hate you?"

Okay, when he puts it that way, it does sound silly. But I've never been in love before; I'm still trying to figure these things out. "No. But you look really, really mad."

The scowl remains on his face. "Then my physical form is adequately expressing my feelings."

I attempt to charm him with a dazzling smile. "What can I do to make you not mad at me anymore?"

I squeal when his arms swoop down and lift me off the floor. He tosses me lightly onto my bed. I thought it was going to hurt since my wings are still here, but it feels like landing on a down pillow. These things are surprisingly comfortable.

Looking down at me with a decidedly less angry face, Kallen says, "I would ask you to promise never to do it again, but I believe you to be too pig-headed to actually follow through with that."

I can't help but laugh. "Gee, thanks."

Stretching out next to me on the bed, he props himself up on his elbow and strokes the feathers of the wing closest to him. "You scared me near to death when you suddenly had wings. I thought you had died."

I nod. "I think everyone did. I even asked the other Angels that when I first met them."

His scowl is gone, and the smallest of smiles touches his lips. "As I said before, you certainly do keep life interesting."
I understand now he was more scared for my safety than angry with me. "I really am sorry. I only did it to keep you safe; I didn't want any of you to get hurt."

"I know," he says as he lowers his head and captures my lips with his in a mind-blowing kiss. No, he's definitely not mad at me anymore.

When he finally lets me up for air, I say, "Want to go flying? I want to test these wings out while I have them."

He chuckles. "I would enjoy watching you try to manage flying."

"Hey," I punch him lightly in the arm. "I flew outside, and I did okay."

Standing up and then offering his hand to pull me up, he says, "We shall see."

Just as we enter the kitchen, the doorbell rings. My parents and grandparents instantly halt their conversation and turn to look at me as if I know who it is. I don't. But I'll find out. Kallen walks with me to the front door and when I swing it open, it's his jaw that drops to the floor.

Standing at the door is one of the tallest women I have ever seen. She's at least as tall as Kallen. Her face is lightly lined with wrinkles, but most seem to be laugh lines. Her skin is tan, but not overly so, and her black hair is salted here and there with gray. It's her eyes that tell me she's a Fairy. No one else has green eyes like that. In fact, they look exactly like Kallen's.

"Grandmother?" is all Kallen says when he finds his voice.

She reaches out and pats his cheek. "Hello, my dear grandson." Turning to me, she holds out her hand. "You are Xandra. My name is Isla, Kallen's grandmother. It is a pleasure to finally meet you."

I put my hand in hers and it looks so small in comparison. "It's nice to meet you, too."

"Your wings are beautiful, may I?" I nod numbly and she reaches out to touch one of my feathers. Bringing her hand back to her side, she says, "Now that you finally know your true destiny, we have a lot of work to do. Are your parents in there?" she asks pointing towards the kitchen. I nod, still dumbfounded.

In astonishment, Kallen asks, "You knew all along, before you sent me here, and you didn't tell me?"

His grandmother grins. "Of course not, you needed to follow your destiny on your own. I simply gave you a little push in the right direction." Turning back to me, she says, "Now, we really must get started, we haven't much time to prepare."

"To prepare for what?" I ask.

She laughs. "Why, to save our realms, of course." She pats me and Kallen both on the shoulder. "You two take a moment to let it all sink in. I'll be in the kitchen with your parents and grand-parents." She walks past us and out of sight into the kitchen.

Kallen and I look at each other. There's obviously no way we're leaving the house now. So, we turn around and follow her to the kitchen.

The Witch Fairy Series

True Of Blood (Witch Fairy Series Book 1)

Blood Prophecy (Witch Fairy Series Book 2)

Blood Lines (Witch Fairy Series Book 3)

Shadow Blood (Witch Fairy Series Book 4)

Blood Of Half Gods (Witch Fairy Series Book 5)

Blood Of Destiny (Witch Fairy Series Book 6)

Blood Of Dragons (Witch Fairy Series Book 7)

Blood Of Egypt (Witch Fairy Series Book 8)

Blood Of Retribution (Witch Fairy Series Book 9)

Blood Of The Exiled (Witch Fairy Series Book 10)

Doppelganger Blood (Witch Fairy Series Book 11)

Blood Of Centaurs (Witch Fairy Series Book 12)

Blood Of Sirens (Witch Fairy Series Book 13)

Elf Blood (Witch Fairy Series Book 14)

Blood And Spirits (Witch Fairy Series Book 15)

Demon Blood (Witch Fairy Series Book 16)

Blood Of The Phoenix (Witch Fairy Series Book 17)

Blood Of Time (Witch Fairy Series Book 18)

Books By This Author

Sanctuary (Sanctuary Series Book 1)

Essence Of Ra (Eliana Brennan Series Book 1)

Exposed (Eliana Brennan Series Book 2)

Homeland (Eliana Brennan Series Book 3)

Sutekh (Eliana Brennan Series Book 4)

Marked (Secrets Of The Djinn Book 1)

Bound (Secrets Of The Djinn Book 2)

Unchained (Secrets Of The Djinn Book 3)